For Rosemary,

Our friendship already spans three decades with more years to come! ☺ 🖤💜

The memories we've shared will always be treasured in my heart, along with you— my dear friend.

Love,
Abi

BARE BONES BENEATH THE FLOORBOARDS

A BOOGER AND BEANS MYSTERY

volume ten

Additional Books by Ali LaVecchia

The Case of the White Knight
Mystery at Mill Creek Bridge
A Zombie on Peacock Hill
A Treasure in Satan's Knoll
The Case of the Mascot's Missing Fire
Voices Beyond the Hidden Staircase
The Ghost on the Front Porch
The Secret in the Old Scrapbook
The Case of the Vanishing Mail

BARE BONES BENEATH THE FLOORBOARDS

A BOOGER AND BEANS MYSTERY

Ali LaVecchia

DEDICATION

To our little pirates, Evie, Fiona, and Cameron, who steal our hearts on a daily basis

A note on pirates:

Pirates date back to the 14th century BC when ocean raiders attacked ships belonging to the Mediterranean and Aegean civilizations. Trade routes were predictable, funneling through narrow channels of water, where ship's thieves patiently waited. These looters managed to move across the Atlantic Ocean over hundreds of years, only to continue their diabolical practices along the east coast of the United States and, eventually, the west coast of Florida. The goods from island adventures and shipwrecks lined the pockets and ships of marauders. Today, many buried treasures still remain undiscovered.

TABLE OF CONTENTS

1

THE DAWN OF EVERYTHING

On the wall-papered walls surrounding me, my blue pin-striped ball players shook their heads at the piles of clothes stacked on my bed. They'd grown accustomed to my adventures in this new house at Mill Creek, more than six months' worth of crazy mixed up mysteries and infrequent teary nights. My mother always says, "If these walls could talk, I wonder what secrets they'd tell." The third baseman and short stop listened to my whispers on the phone late at night with my Grams or with my friends Vito down the street and Booger next door. I'd surely be in the doghouse if those Yankee teammates spilled their guts to Mom.

In my wildest dreams, I never thought I would be so confused about packing for a trip. The only traveling I had ever experienced were for our relocations with my mom, Paulie. After my father passed away in Seattle, which was in March of 2006, the day after the Mars orbiter reached the planet from its prior year's launch at Cape Canaveral in Florida, Paulie made it a point to tell me that we would not stay in the state of Washington any longer. She did not want memories of a fatal crash spoiling our future days together. Dad was a victim of a drunk driver while we were all in the car. My mother lost her baby-to-be, too. I finally understood the traumatic effect it had on her now that I was a month shy of turning fourteen. But it seemed to me that moving to Galveston, Texas, to be with my mom's parents and then to our houses in both Steubenville, Ohio, and now Mill Creek, New Jersey, seemed so much easier than packing for a five-day trip to Sarasota, Florida.

"Honey, you need to shake a leg!" Paulie yelled up from downstairs. "We have to head to the airport in fifteen minutes."

Frustrated, I yelled back, "I know, Mom. I'm trying."

My carryon already had underwear, bras, and socks in it. I even tossed in a pair of decent smelling sneakers that weren't too dirty. The only other footwear I had were on my feet at present – a pair of dollar flip-flops from Columbus Market. Since I knew my tootsies would be cold until we hit the heat in Florida, I tossed socks into my backpack for the plane ride. As I packed, I considered my Grams' advice. First, lay out everything you *think* you want to wear and then edit. At first, I didn't understand. I thought editing only had to do with writing. My mistake. Grams said match things by colors and simplify. Second, bring warm clothes as well as light weight ones. The weather fluctuates in Florida in March, she had explained. When I texted her a minute ago, it was already 71 degrees and climbing but dipped down to fifty-nine at night. Still, those temperatures beat Mill Creek's 30s and 40s along with the threats of more snow and freezing rains.

I already had on my best pair of jeans, black and broken-in, but I rolled up a pair of light blue ones and shoved them into the bag. My Steelers pullover, navy blue zip-up hoodie and plain light green sweatshirt rounded out my choice of tops. Then I narrowed down my T-shirts to three – one white with short sleeves and Middle Creek Middle School printed at the center plus a black one and identical light blue long sleeved pullover, Lululemon brand. The latter was a steal at the flea market at four bucks a pop. Mom told me at dinner last night that I should take less, and if we found we needed something else, we could always buy it when we were at my grandmother's. That was a shocker to me because Paulie was the queen of frugal.

Once I was convinced that I had everything I needed, I tossed my French book and novel from English class on top of everything. The girl on the book cover stared back at me. I hadn't started the book yet but hoped to find out who she was. According to the back cover, *The Book Thief* featured Liesel during Nazi occupied Germany. I figured it tied into the Holocaust, so I was intrigued already. My brain struggled with the notion of putting the book into my bookbag that I was also carrying onto the plane. That way I could start reading it while traveling the two-and-a-half-hour flight. Then I kicked the thought aside, knowing full well that I would try my best to take a nap on the way down. After all, it was 4AM right now, and our flight took off at 6:15. We had a forty-five-minute drive to Philadelphia International Airport where we would stash the car for the next five days then be on our way.

Once again, Paulie's urgent voice traveled up the stairs, "You done yet?" She emphasized the last word then added, "And don't forget to hit the bathroom before we go."

"Okay, Mom," I yelled back. "I'm coming down in a minute."

My fingers rushed to zip up the carryon, and I double checked my bookbag. I threw in an extra pair of mesh running shorts, one more pair of rolled up socks and a long-sleeved gray top with Minnie Mouse on the front. Paulie recommended tucking them in just in case I wanted to change at the airport because of the contrasting weather when we got there. The shirt was a major score at Columbus Market at an indoor kiosk. Two bucks. Made in Indonesia. I had to look it up on our globe to be sure I knew where the country was. Luckily, I was right. Then I dashed into the bathroom, peed as fast as I could, washed my hands then dragged my brush through my mop. I already brushed and flossed so my toothbrush and Glide were already in my backpack. Now, I threw my brush into the mix to join them. With my bag over my shoulder and my carryon in tow, I darted down the steps, two at a time and managed not to fall.

"Car's already warming up," Paulie grabbed two bananas from the hanging mesh bag in the kitchen corner and stuffed them into her oversized handbag.

Curious, I said, "I've never seen that bag before. I'm guessing you got it just for the trip."

She laughed a minute then confessed, "Nope. It's a loaner, Gracie suggested I take it, and I'm glad she did. This sucker can hold a house load of stuff." She opened it to show me the grocery store of random snacks and drinks, "See?"

"Guess we won't starve," I chuckled.

"A girl's got to eat," she nodded and zipped it closed. "You ready to roll?"

"Yeah," I said. "I'm excited. Didn't sleep all that much last night."

"Neither did I," she said, a vision in blue denim leading the way out the side door to our carport. Her auburn hair swung behind her in a bunched-up ponytail. Paulie's hair was one of my own distinct, matching traits from her DNA. According to my mom, my Grams also had auburn hair before coloring her hair once she'd discovered gray and white among her auburn strands. "Whenever I know I have to be up earlier than normal, I set my alarm but always wake up before it even goes off." Then she waited for me to pass, and while I stowed my gear into the opened trunk of her orange Volvo, she locked up our house, carefully muttering, "See you later, house. Be good while we're gone."

I knew we didn't have much to worry about.

Stan Bugerowksi volunteered to keep an eye on our place while we were gone. Living right next door in our duplex made it not only convenient but also easy. Booger's grandmother Babcia and kid sister Haddie would collect our mail. After our last mystery, I was a little wary about the seven-year-old and the mail, but I had to redevelop trust in her. Booger assured me that she had been on her best behavior the last month, mostly because she understood her mistake and made up for it. I believed him because he knew his sister far better than I did.

The trip to the airport was new for me. Darkness shrouded the streets of Mill Creek as we exited town. Only a handful of houses had lights on at the backs of their buildings while a few still had their porch lights on. Either that was deliberate, or they'd been forgotten. Burglaries weren't among the crimes committed in our small town, but people needed to be cautious, regardless. The days of unlocked doors seemed to be over, days Paulette Firenzi Fagioli told me about when she was a child in Seattle. The proximity to Route 206, a remarkably busy highway and main vein from Trenton to Hammonton, could invite strangers who looked to filch expensive items for resale. DVRs, cell phones, loose change in cars, car parts – to name a few. Those low-lifes, motivated mostly by drugs, were addicts. I had heard the stories about the trailer park where Drew's brother lived. Those poor residents were not rich by any means, yet they were an easy target. The trailer homes conveniently sat right off the roadway with many entrances and exits for quick smash and grabs. The bulk of the unsuspecting homeowners there were innocent elderly folks who lived alone and only had monthly Social Security checks to live on. Their fixed income did not welcome thieves.

Route 206 had scattered streetlights along the roadway, and huge tractor trailers that barreled past us on the southbound lane shone their lights right through us. We were only on the road a few minutes before jumping onto Route 38 westbound then Route 295 South. More big rigs accompanied us on the exact same route.

"Geesh," I shouted. "Shouldn't they dim their headlights? I feel like I need to wear sunglasses."

Drat. I thought. I should have grabbed a pair from my top drawer. I knew that the Florida sun would be brighter and stronger than here in New Jersey. Grams warned me about it. Then I totally forgot about them. Oh well. Maybe a Dollar Store down there would offer me a cheap pair.

"I'm used to it, honey. Besides, they're providing a spray of light that helps us, too, until they're on top of us," she flickered her own headlights at them as a reminder for them to dim their high beams. "On top of that, they have deadlines to make, too, just like us."

Confused, I asked, "Whaddaya mean?"

When she reached the Walt Whitman Bridge, she adjusted her own headlights before creeping up over the Delaware River. We were following a short line of both semi-trailers and pickup trucks heading into Philadelphia.

"I'll bet my bottom dollar that the guy in front of us is dropping off cargo at the docks right across the bridge. He'll turn right at the traffic light when we cross over to jump onto I-95." she smiled. "He's got a refrigeration unit. Usually, produce, but who knows."

"What makes you think that?"

"See his license plate? His tags are Florida ones. Bet there are oranges or grapefruits inside for the supermarkets," Paulie remarked, assuredly. "No doubt he's been driving all night long. It's as long as eighteen hours if he's coming up from the citrus groves.

"Man, no sleep!" I exclaimed. "I can't even imagine not having sleep." Then my mind went off the deep end. "Gees, how do they go to the bathroom?"

Her laughter was unanticipated, "Sorry, don't mean to laugh, but they do have a bunch of truck stops along the major highway. They'll stop for a short power nap if they need it. But most truckers pack food, coffee, and Gatorade for themselves plus an empty coffee can to pee in, just so they can save time."

"Ewwwww," I choked and gasped. "That's so gross."

"Facts are facts, honey," was all she said right before she moved into the right lane, just beyond the EZ Pass toll. The trucker in front of us led the way, and, sure enough, he turned right at the traffic light beyond the exit ramp.

"Told ya so," my mother smiled at me before the light turned green.

A quick glimpse at the signage on the side of his truck revealed the eighteen wheeler's company. Florida Citrus Country. A massive splash of oranges served as a backdrop to the lettering. Suddenly, I had an unexpected desire for a glass of freshly squeezed orange juice.

We passed by the Linc, the home field for the Philadelphia Eagles. Then followed a nonstop run of billboards advertising the Atlantic City casinos, Tastycakes, Philly Pretzels, legal advisors, specially designated low-economy parking lots and a gentleman's club called Undercover. I was not sure what that meant, but I didn't care to ask.

"Say, Mom," I questioned. "Is this the same highway you were talking about before?"

Paulie nodded, "Precisely the same. It's our last route, right to the airport now. Runs up and down the east coast. Only about five minutes to go before we park."

Just as she said that, I spotted a green sign with white lettering, *Philadelphia International Airport.* Below it in yellow, an additional message announced, *Exit Only*. I could feel my heart flutter a moment in anticipation again.

Paulie clicked along, carefully maneuvering the lanes around slower traffic. We continued along our way with my well-experienced taxi driver mother avoiding potholes from the winter's beating. Her concentration indicated to me a sense of urgency, trying to get to the parking garage quickly now. We followed the signs to *Arrivals* which confused me, but Mom explained how the parking levels as well as cell phone lot were in that direction. It was all about returning home in the long run.

Once we turned into the long-term garage, a man in a security coat approached us before we pressed the button on a machine at the gate for an entrance ticket, later to be used for payment after we got back from The Sunshine State. He somehow lifted the gate then flagged my mom over to a parking space against the concrete wall near the elevators. There was an orange cone sitting in the middle of it that he removed.

"Thanks, Martell," Mom turned off the engine and pressed the trunk button. I heard the back of the car squeak open. Her body slid out and slammed the door before pulling out the baggage with her friend. "You're aces," she reached into her pocket and pulled out a ten-dollar bill.

"No sense in handing me that, Miss Paulie," the man placed my backpack next to my carryon that already rested on the concrete floor. "You know I won't take it. Not with all the favors you do for me and my family."

Mom stuffed the bill into the front of her khakis and gave him a huge grin, "Well, thanks, just the same."

"Your little cantaloupe will be quite safe right here," the older man patted the hood of the orange Volvo. His eyes were alert, and the whites surrounding his dark pupils seemed lit up in the shadows as he combed the entrance of the building. "When y'all coming back?"

"Not until Friday," Mom tugged out the handle of her bag and piggybacked her smaller bag over it. "My pickup schedule is packed solid when I get back."

Martell shot my mother a smile, "Of course, it is." Then he turned to me, "Your mama is one of the hardest working ladies I know, kid."

I knew that and nodded.

"Well, you two have a wonderful time," he said. "You deserve some time off, woman."

"Don't I know it," was all my mother added before we trotted toward the terminal.

When I peered back over my shoulder, I could barely spot Martell. His skin tone matched the black overalls of his security uniform and heavy black coat. Eerily, only his eyes were flashing through the darkness.

Inside, the building wasn't bustling with crowds. Instead, the line for our Frontier airlines flight was minimal. Paulie had explained to me on our drive over about TSA, short for Transportation Security Administration. She said as passengers we would have to go through a security clearance in order to ride safely in the sky. I had a lot of questions about the whole thing, but my mom, in true Paulie form, didn't hesitate to fill me in. She was always honest and truthful about things I wanted to know.

After the disaster that struck our U.S. soil on September 11, 2001, the government created a department called Homeland Security. It was an agency formed to improve our airport security procedures. I knew nothing about the occurrence or Homeland Security. After all, I was born in 2002. But reading about hijackers who trained on our own country's soil to turn around and use planes against us in an attack on the World Trade Center in New York City, the Pentagon and almost the Capitol in Washington, D.C., was frightening to hear about. My stress level was already at an eight out of ten, having never flown in an airplane before. But now I think I was at a ten out of ten. It didn't seem possible to me that people outside of our country wanted to kill us. A terrorist attack, as the government called it, wasn't something new, but the success of what the Islamic terrorists accomplished was nothing short of amazing and clever. Terrorism was a term I'd heard Mr. Jeffreys, my teacher, talk about in my social studies class, but never in reference to our United States of America.

Fortunately for my sake, Mom assured me that we'd be perfectly safe. All the measures used at airports were showing an excellent history in preventing another such attack.

There was a family of four in front of us along with two young couples. They removed their shoes and put their laptop computers into a bin. The father of the family took a small round tray and popped his watch, car keys and change into it. I wasn't too sure why they were doing all of it, but Paulie whispered as she stood behind me, "I'll fill you in after. You're okay. Just put your bags up when it's your turn."

My mother handed the agent our boarding passes and her identification before I walked ahead. Another agent waved me forward after pointing at my feet. Reaching down, I slipped out of my flip-flops and stacked one on top of the other in my left hand. Then the agent emphatically stressed that I place them on the rollers that led to a screening machine. The entire process was confusing but fascinating. Once I walked past the person viewing the Xray machine, a different agent, a grumpy lady who needed some coffee barked at me, "Your computer! You did NOT take out your laptop. Read the sign." She punched her index finger in its direction then shook her head at me. After closer inspection by the young guy on the other side, the same woman yelled at me, "Pick up your stuff! Hurry it up. We don't have all day, you know." Regardless of her nasty demeanor, I politely thanked her and grabbed my bags. "Shoes! Shoes!" she barked again. My hands reached for my flip-flops then, almost tumbling over my bags, I lurched forward.

"You okay?" the young guy by the machine's aperture said to me. He could have been an older brother of my friend Saul. They looked identical, just one older and the other, younger. "Here, let me help you."

"Yup," I declared, fully embarrassed as I toted my gear over to a metal bench. The rungs were cold to my bottom while my cheeks felt warm from embarrassment. "I just need a moment," I spieled as I sucked in a deep breath to keep calm.

Mom spoke up, "She's new to all of this." She explained, "Her first airplane trip."

"Awesome," the guy beamed at me. "You're going to love it! Have a great trip."

I lifted my head from zipping in my laptop and mumbled, "Thanks. I hope so."

"Nothing to be nervous about," he added, lifting Mom's bag off the processing line. "Here ya go, ma'am."

"Appreciate it," was all Paulie replied before leading me toward our gate.

"Seriously, miss," the young man added as I shuffled forward. "Your first flight is always a great memory. Exciting and scary, all at the same time. But it's fun. And I'm telling you. Once you fly, you'll want to travel more and more in the future. Mark my words." His sincere smile reminded me of Vito, my black-haired Adonis. Warm, courteous, and pure, all wrapped in one. What a combination. Saul's complexion and dark eyes with Vito's pitch-black hair. I think I had a temporary crush. "Have fun!"

We passed a few restaurants that were closed. Then there was a small convenience store with stands of magazines and books, cold boxes of drinks and a handful of odds and ends. Only one small kiosk nearby was lit up, dolling out fresh cups of coffee, bottles of water and snacks. Since Mom couldn't bring her morning thermos of coffee, some rule about nothing more than three ounces for liquids through TSA, we rolled our carry-on bags down the roped off lines and ordered her a large black cup of medium roast. Nothing fancy. And a bargain at under two dollars.

Then with an hour to spare, we found two empty seats near our gate. Seventeen gates existed in Concourse E. Mom pointed out where ours was located among the other competing airlines – JetBlue and Southwest. Gate 4 was our immediate destination. Next stop, sunny Sarasota.

Airport furniture wasn't the most comfortable, I soon discovered. The dull gray leather seats, if they were leather, had very little padding against my back and under my butt. The individual spots were strung together in groups of threes and fours with a small square, floating table connecting them. Skinny arm rests jutted out at both sides, but like the movie theatres, suggested a wrestle between sharers. Being half asleep still, I plopped my bookbag under my chair then wadded up my jacket to use as support behind my back and head. That way I could slouch a bit with my legs extended and propped up on my upended carry-on. My plan was to rest a bit. Besides, the airport felt stuffy and overheated. Paulie supported my decision to stretch out while she spent time on her cell phone with booking new riders and confirming reservations with others before she returned home. She was industrious, never skipping a beat about making money for the two of us.

"Hey, your phone's going off," Mom nudged me on the elbow.

Having fallen asleep for a power nap of my own like the long road truckers, I blindly reached down for my bookbag and fished inside the mesh side pocket. I peeked through the slits of my eyes to see practically every seat around us filled with a living, breathing human being. Where on earth did they all come from?

"It's Grams," I said, clicking on the green call slide. "Yeah, Grams. What's up? We're at the airport. Mom said we should be boarding any minute now."

"Great news, honey," Grams excitedly proclaimed. "So, your flight's on time still."

"Yes," Paulie said loudly enough as she overheard the conversation on the other side.

"Fantastic."

"We'll call you as soon as we land at Sarasota-Bradenton Airport. Should be around 8:30ish. Have some breakfast ready for us, will ya, Ma? We'll be famished!"

"You got it," my grandmother told her.

"Okay, Grams," I added. "We'll see you soon."

"One second, honey. I need to tell you something really important."

Her voice suddenly became a whispered breath, slow and deliberate. At once, I realized how she didn't want her daughter to overhear.

"Sure, what is it?"

"I think you're going to have a mystery on your hands down here," she explained. "I've been living in this house for over four years now, and you know me. I love to change things up every so often," her giggle delighted me. "I just had my living room floors redone, and yesterday rearranged my furniture."

I remembered that from the house in Galveston. Her frequent shifts in the indoor scenery used to drive my grandfather nuts. Grams especially liked rearranging the living room, furniture and pillows and knick-knacks, and my grandpa would go through the roof when she especially touched or readjusted his favorite recliner.

"I know you're in a rush, sweetheart," Grams picked up her pace. "But I wanted to mention that I discovered a strange silver sliver jutting out of my floorboards in the parlor. I can't make out what it is, but I'll shoot you a screenshot."

I loved how my grandmother used all the latest terms for stuff, complements of yours truly.

"I tried a pair of tweezers to pry it out, too, but my arthritis wouldn't let my fingers do the work," she sighed, unhappily. "Hopefully, you'll be able to check it out."

"Sure, Grams. Not a problem."

A loudspeaker interrupted my discussion.

"Good morning, passengers. This is our pre-boarding announcement for those who need assistance. In a few minutes, we'll be boarding families with children, veterans, and our Elite members. Please have your boarding passes ready," the man politely finished.

I observed three people rushing up to the courtesy ticket desk then heard them asking about standby seats. When they were turned away by the airline representative, the three wheeled around, only to plop down near my old seat. With arms firmly crossed against their bodies, they looked like they were on strike. Anger instead of disappointment filled their faces.

"Got to go, Grams," I told her, standing up and grabbing my bookbag. Paulie already had her bag, carryon and mine standing at the ready. "Send me the picture when you can. I'll inspect it then do more, hopefully, when I get to your house."

"Okay, honey. Love you. Safe travels. See you soon."

A couple of minutes later, the loudspeaker announced our seating zone. I gathered my belongings and followed my mother's lead, pulling my carryon behind me and fighting with my bookbag. It kept slipping off my shoulder. With my posture being compromised, my alignment was somewhat tilted as I walked down the jet bridge that connected to the plane. My heart was fluttering at top speed, eyes darting around at my ever-changing surroundings.

"Morning," a lady in black dress uniform greeted me. The lanyard dangling from her neck reminded me of Paulie's, but hers had a green and blue cord with identification at its end. "You look a little lost." Her smile was friendly and inviting. "Let me see your boarding pass."

Mom was already a few rows ahead of me while the woman examined the ticket in my hand.

"Go down ten more rows. You're in 10C by the window."

"Thanks," my fingers delicately held the paper information. "This is my first time on a plane."

"Oh, how nice," she said, readjusting the teal scarf tied around her neck. "My name is Holly. If you need anything, you just let us know. This is Julius." Her head gestured at the man standing beside her. He was the same size as her, around five nine, but a little stocky in his charcoal sweater that zipped open at the top to reveal his knotted teal tie.

He reached into his pocket and handed me a small pin of bronze plastic wings, "We're at your service."

"Appreciate it," I said, staggering down the aisle to where my mother had stopped.

Paulie popped her carryon into the bin above our seat row then grabbed at mine to lay it side by side.

"Climb over," Mom instructed me, "And put your bookbag on the floor in front of your seat. Tuck it under. I'll show you."

I sat into my seat and did what I was told.

"All cozy?" she asked, grinning.

"I suppose so," I offered a reluctant response.

"Don't be nervous, honey," Paulie told me. "You'll be just fine."

"Uh huh."

I saw my hands clutching the end of the arms, tightening into a fist like grip.

Holly waltzed down the aisle, reminding everyone to buckle their seatbelts. I hadn't realized that I was sitting on mine. I tugged both sides free from under my rear-end then clipped one into the other. Mom did the same. Julius checked the stowed away gear up above and shut each bin tightly. He, too, looked at our laps to be sure we were buckled in then shot me a thumbs up. I returned the favor.

Suddenly, there was a buzzing coming out of my bookbag.

Grams.

I unclipped my seatbelt, reached down and grabbed the phone.

"You're going to have to shut that off," Julius warned me before heading back toward the pilot's cabin. His voice wasn't scolding, merely informative yet his brown eyes stared me down.

Mom gave me a frown. She knew the ropes and apparently had hers already off. I was a newbie, learning the ways of the airlines.

My palms were sweaty and fingers, shaking. But somehow, I managed to unlock my screen. A text message awaited.

Here's the picture was all it said. Attached was a photo.

Eyes squinting to examine the details, I held the phone close to my face.

Exactly as my grandmother had mentioned. A sliver of silver appeared. The shiny spot between two floor planks wasn't big at all. Maybe an inch or more. I stared at it for a few more seconds then shut off my phone when Paulie gave me a poke in the ribs with her elbow.

Without a closer look, I couldn't imagine what it could be.

2

MAKING A RUN FOR IT

Regardless of my phone blowing up, I lingered in bed and gradually peeled the covers off around 10:00. Why I thought I'd escape Beans once she went off on a vacation was beyond me. I should've known better. I'd heard of the term *staycation*, and, other than track practice, I intended to have lazy days for an entire week.

A spray of sun rays peeked through the edges of my pulled shades. On a cold winter's day, the natural light lifted my spirits. Suffice it to say, I'd do a short run before pigging out in the kitchen. No doubt, my grandmother would have a feast ready for me, knowing that I wouldn't be rushing out the door for the bus. I could already detect the smell of bacon creeping up through the heat vent when I stood peeing at the toilet. One piece would fuel my short thirty- minute escapade through the neighborhood.

My favorite black sweatpants sat at the top of the dirty clothes heap. I changed into fresh boxer briefs and sniffed my choice before pulling my sweats over my bare legs. Then I popped open my bottom dresser drawer to grab the only clean hoodie I had. There was a reason why it remained alone in the drawer. It didn't zip up. Instead, it pulled over my head and felt tight around my neck. I wasn't thrilled with the Shoprite logo on it either. The white background to the screaming yellow and red looked decent with the white stripe on the outside of my pant legs, and I could tolerate wearing it for a half an hour.

I checked the temperature on my cell phone.

51 degrees. Decent for a brisk morning run.

"Morning, Babcia. Morning, Haddie," I yelled as I bounded down the stairs.

"Balthie," Babcia chirped from the kitchen. Her profile was backlit by the sun through the kitchen door at the back of the house. Her body hunched forward, no doubt sipping her second cup of vanilla tea with honey and lemon. "You sleepyhead boy. Sleep, sleep, sleep."

I heard my kid sister giggle behind me. She was on the couch, tapping away at the screen on her pink Kindle. Engrossed in one of her favorite games, Haddie's little fingers occasionally picked up the cinnamon bun besides her and without looking, found her mouth and took a quick squirrel-like nibble. Then she'd smack her lips, drop the bun back in her Dora the Explorer dish and proceed to click away. Haddie's teacher suggested to my dad and other parents before Christmas that her students with autism should own a Kindle for Kids, a child's version of an iPad. These mini-computers designated for children offered games and learning activities. The mental stimulation with the games on it first began as small rewards for Haddie and her classmates. My sister was one of them who enjoyed using the machine and responded well to it. So, my dad got one for her as a Christmas present, the exact color and type used in her school classroom. Haddie was over the moon when she opened it. And before she ripped open the other toys and clothes stacked under the tree that morning, her little body, all clad in her purple My Little Pony pajamas and tiny white ankle socks, scurried off to the dining room table to turn it on and play. The pings and dings made her smile as she navigated the screens. Thank goodness Santa Claus remembered to charge it ahead of time. At present, Haddie was fully engaged just like Christmas morning. Having finished clearing the breakfast dishes and placing them into our dishwasher, Babcia handed her the Kindle for completing her chore.

I strolled over to Haddie and kissed her bob of chestnut brown hair.

"Good morning, sweet pea," I told her, pushing my head between the Kindle and her face. Her eyes redirected themselves into mine and blinked hard. When she was a toddler, she would always do the same, acknowledging I was there. Nothing more. "Sorry to interrupt you, Haddie." I tapped her head and shuffled into the kitchen. "Carry on!"

"You eat now?" my grandmother began to slide off her seat and head to the counter.

"Naw, Babcia," I told her, plucking a slice of crispy bacon from the plate in front of her. "This will hold me over until I get back."

"No good, Balthie," her face contorted as she scolded me. Wisps of her graying hair peered out from the edges of the matching babushka swaddling her head. "You run now? Boy needs food. Boy needs energy," her wizened finger wagged in front of my face. "Cold outside. Wear coat," she pointed now at my winter jacket clinging off the rack by the front door. "Put on! Father will be angry. Tell Babcia no good."

Like Haddie, I bent over and kissed my grandmother on top of her head, "Dad won't yell at you, Babcia. He knows I do things my way, especially when it comes to working out. I can't run with heavy clothes on. That's all there is to it," I explained. "But don't you worry. I won't be out all that long. Just thirty minutes. Be back in no time."

Her frail hands coated in tiny brown spots lifted the neighboring plate and turned it upside down to cover the scrambled eggs and bacon. Babcia didn't believe in wasting aluminum foil or Saran Wrap. All the while, my grandmother shook her head back and forth, clicking her tongue at me and mumbling something in Polish. I could only imagine the choice words she was saying to me. But I wasn't about to ask for a translation.

A slight breeze welcomed me when I unlocked our front door. The coolness in the air reminded me of an early spring morning. As I stepped off the front steps, I could immediately feel the warmth of the sun on my face. I pulled out my knit cap from my pocket and tugged it snugly on my skull. Babcia surprised me with it in my Christmas stocking. It provided a ton of warmth. Its scarlet color with the squishy white pompom on top made my noggin look like a radish. But it was a necessity, ample enough protection from the winter's cold on previous days outside. It was now my "go to" head covering. I didn't care what it looked like to anyone else. Babcia's gift of love was the by-product of her church ladies' group where she learned the basics of knitting and purling. . . . or as she called it, "knit a pearl." My fingers discovered my black gloves deep inside my front pouch. I'd forgotten they were there as I tucked my phone in their place. I set the timer on my watch and headed in the direction of the lumber yard.

Mill Creek was bustling for a Monday morning. Ida Meyer swept dirt away from the bakery's *Welcome* mat at its front door and caught my eye. With a quick wave, she said hello then went back to brooming. Even though I knew a warm breakfast awaited my return at home, I knew I had to stop in for a sticky bun. Babcia wouldn't mind, especially if I gave her and Haddie a piece from it.

As I turned the corner onto Brook Bend, I spotted Mr. Naylor chatting with a trucker. The two men were fastening and tightening broad straps across a massive load of planks in the lumber yard. Their breath turned to frosty puffs as they bantered and laughed while they worked. Then another man, burlier and ruddy faced, approached the truck cab, climbed aboard, and settled behind the steering wheel. He gave me a nod then proceeded to turn over the engine. His lean, lanky partner gave the final strap at the back a good tug then shook Mr. Naylor's hand before jumping up into the cab. I cautiously waited and watched to determine which direction the truckers were headed. Noticing, Mr. Naylor signaled for me to stay put. The end of the cargo bed moved slowly, backing up fifty feet over the loose gravel before lurching forward to the right, aiming for the road where I stood, dead center. Quickly, I moved onto the sidewalk to the left of me, nearing the alleyway that ran behind the bakery. Once the truck moved past me, I continued running on the empty pavement. Its even surface allowed for my feet to remain stable, an important consideration having fully recuperated from my ankle injury a few months before. I wasn't about to go down that path again. I hated being cooped up and sedentary. The waiting game of healing was a royal nuisance.

I decided to stay straight a few more blocks until I turned left onto Ash Lane. That led to the section of Main Street where Colin Malloy's house stood. The estate itself took up a full block, the mansion stretching almost to its fullest extent. I'd never truly seen the inside, other than the kitchen and a peek into the sitting room beyond it when I spoke to Old Man Malloy weeks before he died. Only Colin lived there now, alone, ever since his father passed away last year. Colin probably spent less time there than before, having somewhat moved in with Aunt Gracie. She was Vito's relative who owned the variety store on the corner of Mill and Main Streets. Call it gut instinct, but I neither liked nor trusted Colin Malloy. His dealings as a real estate broker and Wall Street investor never seemed honest to me. Maybe it was the words that my dad spilled into my ears over time that influenced my opinion. He respected and liked Old Man Malloy, but not his son. Nor did he like how Colin, his only child, treated the old man. He seemed selfish and neglectful, greedy and egotistical. So, maybe my distaste for the man who was more than polite to me and appeared quite kind to Vito's aunt was based on my father's opinion only. I felt a little bad about that, but not enough to change my opinion. At least, not for now.

I watched the property for a minute as I neared it and observed red backup lights moving out of the driveway. Colin Malloy was exiting his domicile in his silver Porsche and heading to whereabouts unknown. I waited until he spun out onto the street then crossed the blacktop. He didn't even notice me. He was a man on a mission.

About fifteen minutes now into my run and heading in the direction of Mill Creek Bridge, my phone went off. Did I even need to check it?

Beans.

I figured I'd call her after breakfast, but I guessed after so many text messages, I'd better answer.

"Yeah, what's up?"

"Is that anyway to greet somebody?" Beans voice was impatient and curt with me.

"Sorry," I huffed, sucking the cool air into my lungs but not stopping my jog. "I'm finishing up a run."

"Well, you could've called me before you started," she reminded me. "I've sent you half a dozen messages."

As if I didn't know that.

I took another deep breath and slowed down my pace so I could talk better, "Got a late start." Why I had to explain anything to her was beyond me. "I slept in. Felt great."

There was silence on the other end. When she was good and ready, she spoke up again, "I sent you a picture. Did you get it?"

"Yeah. I saw it."

"Well?"

"Well, what?" I said, annoyed that I was almost fast walking now.

"Did you try to zoom in on it?"

"Didn't have time," I told her which was the truth. I didn't think it seemed all that important when I woke up. Heck, I hadn't even given time to breakfast or Babcia or Haddie for that matter. "I'll check it out when I get home. What's the rush?"

Her voice rattled with disgust, "What's the rush? You exasperate me!" The puffs of air that she emitted warned me that she was dead serious and wasn't playing around. "I haven't been able to investigate it yet because my Grams decided to stop on the way home from the airport to treat us to breakfast. Some place called the Waffle House."

"Oh," was all I added, knowing nothing I said would avoid an argument, and I was in no mood for it. I was having a peaceful run until this second. "Sounds decent."

"I'll send you more photos once we're at Grams' house," she continued. "But maybe you can share the picture with Vito and see what he thinks so far."

I knew what Vito would think. He'd think, "This isn't much to go on. I need more details, better photographs with clear, sharp images." Then he'd follow up with a need for evidence from the surroundings.

In my mind, I wouldn't bother him until I had those things ironed out. Otherwise, it'd be a waste of his time and mine.

"Sure," I said, merely appeasing her.

"You promise?" she urged. "Don't brush me off."

"I'm not," I said, knowing full well that I was. "But I'll let him know for ya. Now can I finish my run, please?"

"Okay. But promise."

"I promise."

"Pinky swear?"

"Oh, for Pete's sake," I moaned.

"Say it," she barked into the phone. "Say it!"

"All right. All right. I pinky swear! Geesh!"

I noted the time on my phone. I only had ten more minutes to go before eating, and I suddenly realized I was starving. My stomach was grumbling at me as a reminder.

"All righty," her voice became happy and light in contrast. "Call me after lunch. I'll see what else I can get to send you. I already sent the other picture to Vito, too, but I haven't heard back from him either."

Brother! I thought. I couldn't believe that she was already torturing my buddy on his day off, too. I knew he had practice at our high school since we'd shared schedules. With football season done, Vito kept busy training and was gearing up for baseball season with his teammates. It wasn't unusual for high school athletes to be involved in multiple sports throughout the year even if one particular team sport outweighed the others. Football was Vito's hopeful route to a scholarship to college where he would study forensics science. As for me, I continued my upper body workouts even when my foot recuperated. But now, I logged short easy runs with my revitalized body but did weight training after school. With our brief February hiatus, I'd do some of that at home in my bedroom. I had two light weight kettle bells and a couple ten and fifteen pound dumbbells. They would do the trick until I got back onto the Nautilus machines in the weight room linked to the gym.

Since my foot seemed to be holding up quite well, I decided to add an extra two miles to my route. Turning right onto Cobblestone Lane led me to the empty playground at the elementary school, the one that Haddie attended. I was surprised to see Daisy Dukes there with her two little girls, all bundled up in heavy coats with furry hoods tied up around their faces. They gripped the chrome bars in front of them on the merry-go-round while their mother side-straddled the wooden seat and pushed her booted foot on the frozen ground. High pitched giggles warmed the brisk air, telling me her daughters were loving every minute of their spinning. Daisy Dukes smiled and nodded hello to me to which I flagged my palm in her direction. The young twenty- or thirty-year-old mother dug in and sped up her propelling foot while I proceeded to the dead end of the lane and curved around to the left.

My eyes landed on the old black hearse behind Donaldson's Funeral Home. Young Artie, another thirty-something old was Mr. Donaldson's assistant. He was opening the double doors at the back of the lengthy vehicle and sliding out a gurney. The flat bed extended enough to lower its back wheeled legs onto the cement landing pad. I'd only seen that familiar piece of equipment when Babcia had to be transported to the hospital. She'd fractured her hip last summer and suffered in a lot of pain. The sight of the gurney unnerved me, bringing back the scary memory of seeing an ambulance parked outside our house and my poor grandmother crying as they loaded her, all alone and frightened to death.

"Yo," Artie's eyes settled on me. "How's it going, bro?"

"Good, Artie. I'm good. You?"

"Can't complain," his hands reset the dead body in the middle of the moving platform. Once he had the covering tightly tucked around the corpse, he shut the hearse's heavy black doors. "Well, I could, I guess, but nobody would listen," then he started giggling, sounding like a slow chugging locomotive.

"I suppose," I said, not laughing at his weak attempt at a joke. "Who's the poor soul?"

"Not sure. Still being identified." Artie shook his shaggy brown head then pulled up the waistband of his drooping pants. Their khaki hems balanced upon the top of his greenish brown duck shoes. "Bad crash out in the country, near the intersection of Route 206 and Pemberton Road. Hit the traffic light pole. Died on impact."

I hated hearing that. There were times when the noise from a bad accident on 206 could be heard in our house during the summer nights with our windows wide open. Our home was situated less than a mile away from that intersection. When tractor trailers came barreling down the major highway at night, trying to make deadlines, they'd zoom through the light. Didn't matter if it was amber, green or red. Then some unsuspecting driver in a drunken haze would get nailed. I was wondering if that was the case today.

"Awful" was all I could utter.

"Yeah, dude looks like he was only in his twenties. Life gone too soon."

"You're telling me."

How could I not agree? Not that I wanted to admit it, but I expected people to pass in their old age – maybe 80s and 90s – that was the norm. When I heard about anybody younger, it spooked me. Even hearing about Quinn's father's death in his thirties bugged me. He didn't even have a shot at experiencing lots of what life had to offer, especially for him, his wife, and his young daughter. Beans didn't speak much about it. I knew it pained her still and even her mother. Paulie put up a good front. My dad and I could tell that she was a lonely woman, filling her days with unlimited hours in her private cab service. And whenever Mrs. Fagioli was around my dad, I could see how she missed the company of a man close to her own age.

While I watched Artie drag the gurney up the ramp and into the back hallway of the funeral home, I felt a thud against my back.

"Dude!"

Vito.

"Whaddaya on a break or something?" his laugh was loud and menacing.

His running attire matched mine. However, his head sported a forest green baseball cap with ear flaps attached. A line of white cord dropped below his ears, reminding me how Vito always ran with his music. I usually did, too, but I forgot to grab my iPod that was in my backpack.

He kept running in place as I spoke to him, "I was planning to call you later, man. Whatcha up to later on?"

"Not much, really." His lower teeth pulled in his lower lip while he watched me.

"Well, guess who wants me to show you something? Another mystery unfolding?"

"Ummmmm," his eyes twinkled. "Not much of a challenge with that question."

"I know, right?" I tried to sound apologetic. "That girl never quits. Wherever she goes, she discovers some kind of dramatic scenario. Like she is radar, drawn to it or something."

"You know, you are right about that. She seems like she has a built-in magnet." With a tilt of his head, he began to rub his hands together. "Do I even want to know what it is this time?"

Because he was still running, my body began to unconsciously mirror his movements. I explained to him how it would be easier to swing by his place after I grabbed breakfast and show him the one and only photo that I had on my phone. Easy to accommodate, my friend agreed. I had a sneaking suspicion that this new adventure for Beans would be a bust, and then she'd be so bummed out that she'd bug me about that, too.

It was a no-win situation.

3

A SILVER LINING

Only two small fluffy squares remained dead center on my plate. They were swimming in a huge puddle of maple syrup and teasing my tastebuds. As hungry as I was, I wanted to take my sweet time, savoring the moments I had left to finish mopping them around before sliding them into my mouth. Paulie lifted an orange thermal pitcher and streamed a little more coffee into her mug then offered Grams more, too. Gently, Grams placed her hand over the top of her white rim, signaling Mom, "No, thanks."

"Aren't you going to finish that waffle?"

"Oh, sure, Grams," I shook my head at her. "I'm just taking a short break then I'll delight in my final two bites. I've never heard of a Belgian waffle before. These suckers are enormous." I held my plate up to my eyeballs. "And they're so thick but light. You know?"

The special of the morning was topped off by a heaping pile of fresh chopped strawberries and major dollops of whipped cream. To top it off, the waitress brought out my orange juice, probably freshly squeezed at a local orange grove nearby. Grams said there were still loads of them dotting the Sarasota area even though others had been farmed out to developers. New houses were rising all over the place.

"Why don't we have any Waffle Houses up our way?" I finally surrendered to my fork in hand and stuck the tines into the smaller of the two pieces. As it came up to my lips, I licked the edges to make it last.

"There are plenty of fast-food restaurants up our way, but not everything around the country comes as far east or north," Paulie lifted the typical coffeehouse mug to her lips and slowly sipped her hot coffee. "For example, Chick-Fil-A came up to New Jersey from Atlanta. And Cracker Barrel is from Tennessee."

"Woah," I said. "I had no idea."

"Sure," Grams added, slurping the end of her coffee then reaching for her glass of water.

She took her napkin and dabbed the corner into it before applying it to a spot on her turquoise blue top. Apparently, a drip of brown managed to escape her mouth and land above one of the arms of a gold starfish. There was a circle of three sea creatures beneath her neckline – a papa starfish, a mama starfish, and a baby star, in descending order within a curling ocean wave with white suds. "How about Kentucky Fried Chicken? That was from a remote town in Kentucky, right?"

"Yes, Mom," Paulie grinned. "There are many, Quinn."

"In fact," Grams added, "We're even starting to get some of your stores and restaurants down this way."

"Really," I said, swallowing piece number one and replacing it by its final friend.

"Sure," my grandmother nodded. "We now have around three Wawa's in Sarasota. I loved that place up by you and was thrilled when they opened up down here. One is not far from my house."

Mill Creek, New Jersey, had about four Wawa's near it, too. The one closest to us on Route 206 was a Super Wawa because it had gas pumps available for drivers, not just coffee, sandwiches, and snacks. Any time of the day, I would see a line of cars zooming in and out of the parking spaces. Often, the drivers left their vehicles standing empty by the pumps while rushing inside the store to grab a cup of coffee.

"Wow," I said, squashing the delicate waffle with my molars. "I'm not kidding. This is the BEST darned waffle I've ever had in my life." I swept my napkin from my lap and smeared it across my face. "That hit the spot. I didn't realize I was so hungry."

Grams slid her hand onto mine, "I figured as much, sweetheart. And you two were up mighty early. No time to eat. Just time enough to race to the airport and jump onboard." Grams took her napkin from her hand and wadded it into a little clump of paper. Remnants of ketchup red dotted the edges from her meal of scrambled eggs. I didn't get it, and it grossed me out whenever I saw Grams use ketchup at our house on her eggs. I was a plain Jane, I suppose, eating my eggs plain, no salt, no pepper, just as is but runny enough to dip my crispy toast points. Sweet ketchup on eggs made no sense to me at all. "Have you two thought about what you want to do first while you're here, staying with me? We have lots of time to cover a lot of territory," her face lit up with a broad grin and her eyes twinkled with mischief.

"Well, I do want to explore that photo you texted me," I said, almost in a whisper. I knew my mom probably knew about it, sitting in such close proximity on the plane while I finished studying it then powering down my phone.

Paulie's eyes whirled in their sockets.

"Honestly, Quinn!" she started. "Can't you for once stop thinking about another mystery? We're on vacation, honey. Time for just the three of us. No drama."

To add a poignant punctuation mark, Mom somewhat slammed her empty coffee mug onto the booth's tabletop. Her auburn hair got retied back into a low ponytail, a sign that she truly was annoyed with me. She did things like that to let me know that she was exasperated, totally losing her cool with me.

Grams noticed and jumped to my defense, "We have plenty of time for that, my Jersey girl." Her eyes locked with my mother's as she continued, "But we'll do anything your little heart desires. After all, you are my guests, and your wishes are my command."

Paulie groaned, loudly then flagged our server for our check so we could be on our way. I watched as her arm reached under the table to the floor where her pocketbook rested. But before she tugged it up onto her lap, my mom readjusted the green sleeves of her windbreaker, pushing them up to her elbows. Another gesture that she was super irritated with me.

At that moment, I saw my Grams give me a shushing index finger to her lips and a wink. That meant she was on the same page that I was. She'd help me in my new adventure behind Paulie's back. Grams was always on my side, and that drove my mother insane. We were two peas in a pod.

The trip to my grandmother's house was a short ten minutes. Clark Road was a main artery, crossing a southern section of Sarasota from west to east. Grams explained that there were many similar roadways intersecting the region – University Parkway, the one we'd used to Route 75 from the airport; Fruitville Road and Bee Ridge Road. Then there were Honoré, MacIntosh, Beneva, Tamiami Trail and a bunch more that she rattled off, ones that moved north to south. The names were definitely unique to the area, a far cry from what Mill Creek had to offer with its jewels, flowers, trees and the mundane, like Main Street. Signage everywhere opened my eyes to even more. I couldn't pin names down to nature only since Native American labels fell upon routes as well. Grams said that Tamiami Trail, for example, was a really old route that ran from Tampa all the way south to Miami, and that the name no doubt was from the Miccosukee Indians. They were part of the Creek Nation who migrated to Florida from the west and hid out in the Everglades during the Indian Wars. She said that was during the 1800s. To top it off, Grams mentioned that they were one of the oldest tribes who existed on American soil pre-Christopher Columbus, the explorer.

Leave it to my grandmother to know about these Native Americans. I only knew about the Lenni-Lenape that occupied parts of New Jersey, Pennsylvania, and Delaware. Books about them often fashioned the tops of the bookshelves in our middle school library. My Grams was a wealth of knowledge. She knew a little about everything. Now I realized where my mother got it from. Their DNA loved history and all sorts of odd and end trivia. It was no wonder that I was following in the same suit.

"I think the name is a portmanteau," my mom chimed in.

"What's a port whatchamacallit?" I asked, never hearing that word before. "It sounds French."

Mom grinned at me over the back of her passenger seat while Grams laughed, "You're right, hon. Port is from porter – to carry – in the French language."

I knew that wasn't right, but I didn't want to correct my grandmother. I had too much respect for her, but I knew my French language well. "A transporter" translated into "to carry" in French.

Shaking my head, "I thought maybe it had to do with door or doorway. Porte. P – O – R – T – E," I spelled it proudly. My French at school was better than ever, even tutoring Booger through his roadblocks in the language at high school. He hated it while I loved it. It sounded so rich and smooth. Not only that, but it also sounded romantic to me. "Translation could be 'door to Miami.' Something like that."

Grams layered in her own dialogue, "You're quite a clever young lady. You know that?"

"I've been told," I said, matter of fact, mostly by Booger's former babysitter, Granger, and my own grandmother.

"Anyway, a portmanteau is a combination of words. In this case, Tam would represent Tampa and overlap into Miami or Tam + Miami = Tamiami."

My brain was on high alert now, thinking I'd see a bunch more on the green and white road and street signs. Right now, however, I couldn't remember a single one.

"So, would brunch be one? A combination of breakfast and lunch," I pondered.

"Yup, that's correct!" Mom said.

"And let's throw in smog while we're at it," Grams added. "Smoke + fog = smog."

"Portmanteau," I repeated to myself.

What a terrific word.

Grams suddenly threw on her blinker to turn off Clark and right onto Swift Road.

"Need to make a quick pit stop. We're going out of our way a little bit, but the post office is up this way and I want to get some stamps plus check my mailbox."

"You don't have a mailbox at your house?" I wondered. "Doesn't anybody have one around here?" the notion was unnerving. "We get our mail delivered at our house."

The seventy-something woman blurted out a huge laugh, deep from within her belly, "No, Beans. We all have mailboxes for the most part. I just have a separate mailbox for business inside the post office. I have to pay rent on it every month, but I keep it for packages and business mail."

I really wasn't that curious about it anymore. That didn't matter to me. I was too busy soaking up all the plants and trees and flowers and stores. My surroundings were a confusion of magical plants, tall and fluffy or short and bushy. Yet an assortment fooled me with their prickly points and straight blades like knives. Then there were the people. Everybody was sporting a tank top and shorts, long to the knees or tightening high around their thighs. A handful of women walked the sidewalks in sundresses that fell at the knees, or surprisingly, to their ankles. Their vibrant colors reminded me of the patchwork quilt on the back of Granger's couch, one made from Josephine's clothes from her childhood. Granger treasured that handiwork of his wife, now suffering in a memory facility for Alzheimer's patients.

In the parking lot of the post office, cars and mail trucks buzzed haphazardly in and out of the driveways. Their speed was far too unsafe for pedestrians walking around. Only 9:30 in the morning and traffic even on the streets seemed heavy. An occasional yellow school bus rumbled down the road, and little kids the age of Haddie waved at us through the opened windows. It was hard to get used to the weather difference. I could sense the sweat building up inside my heavier clothing. I couldn't wait to rip them off once our bags were dragged into my grandmom's home.

Grams carted a couple of large envelopes under her arm while juggling a rather large box, the size of a waste basket, in her arms. She popped open the trunk of her light blue Audi wagon and placed them all on the floor as I watched. There was that sneaky wink again. Grams was up to something, and it surely had to do with us or maybe just me. I was hoping for the latter.

We headed out once more up Swift and onto the other side of a circle, or as Paulie told me, a roundabout, where it renamed itself Tuttle. The name of the street changed. Back home, we had a few like that, too. It always made me wonder if a council member or businessmen in town duked it out to have their own family name on a street, only to back down and settle for splitting it this way. Funny to consider.

Then suddenly, we were driving on a street called Bahia Vista. Paulie asked her mother if it led west to Sarasota Bay. Grams nodded.

"Let me guess," I chimed in. "Bahia means bay."

"Bingo!" my Grams yelped then flipped her blinker on before turning right.

But after her mistake with the French word for carry, I wasn't so sure she was right.

Before we fully turned onto the street, my head cocked around to keep watch on a small family band, maybe four men, two women and about five kids. Both women and children had white bonnets on their heads, resembling Daisy Duke's littlest girl. The ties were snugly beneath their chins and dresses of periwinkle blue fell to their feet. Some wore white sneakers while others had on open-toed sandals. The men, on the other hand, were in short-sleeved white shirts, black pants, black suspenders, and casual shoes. On top their heads they balanced straw brim hats, but none that I recognized. The brims were shorter than the larger ones that women wore at the beach. The children mirrored their parents, and the eleven had one thing in common. They all rode three-wheeler bicycles.

"Say, Grams."

"Yes, sweetie?"

"Who were those people? Those men with the beards and the ladies with the bonnets?"

My mom knew and didn't hesitate to answer before Grams, "Amish. They live down here for the winter, some – year around. We have communities of them back home, not in New Jersey but Pennsylvania."

"No kidding!"

"That's right, sweetie peach," Grams nodded. "They have a community nearby called Pinecraft."

"Very cool," I said. "But why do they dress like that?"

Grams took the time to detail the lives of the Amish and the Mennonites. Their handiwork in carpentry and quilt making along with baking and other homemade items made them a valuable commodity in any region. Their work lasted a lifetime. Most of the families came from farming backgrounds, in some cases with no electricity which honored their old-fashioned religious observations. Their transportation back home was basically horses and buggies. And their clothing was handmade without zippers or Velcro closures, all hand sewn to perfection.

"They own and run two very popular restaurants nearby also," Grams continued.

According to her, they'd built them by hand, from the ground up, with their masterful woodworking from the walls and roof to the tables and chairs inside. In fact, she noted that we'd go to one of them tonight for dinner. Yoder's was its name, known for its fried chicken and delicious pies. Yoder was the family name, a common one like Smith or Brown or Jones in America.

"Believe it or not, most of them are snowbirds this time of the year," my grandmother turned onto another short street lined with beautiful pink mimosa trees and towering palms. Lots of flowering bushes, too, lined the perimeters of people's yards. "You know what a snowbird is, right?"

Paulie turned her head and gave me a thumbs up. She'd told me about people from cold wintery spots in the country moving temporarily to warmer spots during winter. In a way, our short vacation at Grams made us snowbirds, migrating to a warmer nest.

"Yup!"

"Well, those folks come down from Ohio, Michigan, Pennsylvania, and other places. Neat, huh?" Grams suddenly jerked the car to the right and into the longest driveway among the other houses. "Here we are! Home, sweet, home."

Her hand turned the key to shut off the engine, and like a bolt of lightning, Grams jumped from the driver's seat, slammed the door, and popped open the back. She grabbed her packages while Paulie and I took our duffle bags from beside me on the back seat along with our backpacks. Outside of the car, I realized that the temperature continued to rise.

"You're both going to want to get out of those warm clothes," she said, already jogging up the bleached white sidewalk.

Her house on Pindo Palm had a big front yard with a few short palm trees squatting on it. They resembled pineapples but with twelve feet tall fanning palm fronds. Their fingers reached outward, embracing the sunny air around them. Patches of wild yellow daisies with reddish centers seemed perfectly centered between the trees along with a handful of blue Salva, a plant we had at the edge of our front porch in Mill Creek. The rest of her yard actively grew regular old grass like we had. Surprisingly, the other houses neighboring her own, had stone lawns, all ivory and beige. Grams' landscaping made her house look like a million bucks, especially since it seemed like an older style rancher, all one floor. Its roofline was flat and looked like it was made of tin or a metal of some sort. It was pitched at about a twenty-degree angle, and a matching one sat a little lower over her single car garage. A creamy teal color coated the outside stucco. Oddly, it matched the color of my grandmother's top. Before following Paulie and Grams to the front door, I did a three sixty, taking in all the other houses. Each one had an unusual color – peach, raspberry, lime green, pink, sky blue and lavender. I thought we were on a Caribbean Island. Maybe that was the plan behind it.

Once inside, the rooms flowed, sprawling wide from end to end. The foyer was open without walls, about three feet wide with one foot by two feet tiles of creamy beige. The outer sidewalk matched it with the landing, making it seem like it was bringing the outdoors, in. Then the open living room and dining room latched together with pale gray, silver, black and ivory planks that flowed in a diagonal pattern and connected directly into the kitchen that had a separate island from the cooking space and double sink. All the cabinets were linen white with shiny nickel color knobs. Stainless steel appliances polished off the perfect look of newness. Refrigerator, oven and stove, dishwasher, microwave, the works.

"Grams, this place looks like it's brand spanking new," I gasped. "How old is this house anyway?"

"It better look saucy," she smirked. "Your mom knows I spent some of her inheritance of redoing everything in this place after your grandfather passed. I needed to erase the bad memories of your grandfather's final years. I felt like this place was a hospital zone with all the contraptions that kept him going. Poor man suffered. Bless his soul and may he rest in peace," and she made the sign of a cross on her torso.

I remembered when my Gramps was sick. He had lung cancer and heart failure. And although he received treatment for both and rallied periodically, he was doomed. Mom didn't visit much during that time, trying to keep the memory of him from healthier days. I knew it broke her heart, but Grams understood. She didn't want Paulie to come around to see him so weak. I also believe that my grandmother didn't want her daughter to see her upset and hurting either. When we lived with Grams and Gramps in Galveston, Gramps was always fishing at the piers or walking me to the ice cream parlor around the corner from their house. We both loved mint chocolate chip and Rocky Road. I'd get my scoop in a pretzel cone while he got his in a waffle cone. Then we'd top them off with a handful of rainbow sprinkles. I loved that man so very much. He always smelled like peppermints because he never went anywhere without those from local restaurants. They sat on the counter near the checkout cashier, and when the cashier said, "Help yourself," he sure would.

"To answer your question, this house was built in the 1970s. But it has sturdy bones, so says the guy that redid all this for me. He and his small crew, all originally from Guadeloupe, are experts in renovations – everything from reconstructing to tiling to painting. You name it. They can do it. They're not afraid to work either. Arrived at daybreak and left at sundown. Usually, I'd give them lunch and drinks. They appreciated it, and I think they did meticulous work because of it . . . along with my added motivation, a generous tip at the end," she laughed. "But your Gramps said you get what you pay for, and you need to always respect people, and they'll respect you back."

When my eyes fell upon my mother's face, she lit up.

"I've heard that one before. Right, Ma?"

"You bet, young lady. Say, Mom," Paulie asked. "Would you mind if I took a shower? Wash some of the travel bugs off me."

"Sure," Grams headed down the hallway to our right. "Back this way. The two guest bedrooms are down here along with your bathroom. You each get your own room. How about that?" my grandmother pursed her lips and blew a kiss in my direction.

Once Paulie and Grams were out of the way, I snooped around. The flooring in the living and dining room were the same as the photo that Grams sent me. But I didn't know where the sliver of silver was located. I sat my backpack on a salmon-colored high-backed stool at the island counter then began my search. The spaces between the faux wood planks were slim because the engineering had them squished tightly up against each other along with a seam of grout. From what I'd observed on current commercials, they were a popular designer's trend. The two vying competitors were interlocking types of flooring or wood-looking tiles. These surely were snug fitting but there was a definite line of grout pulling their look together.

The search seemed impossible, and the clock was running.

I noticed an armchair placed awkwardly out of symmetrical order in the room. Every other piece of furniture was situated in a precise location, but that chair was out of whack. I hustled over, shoving it a little toward the enclosed back porch or lanai as Grams called it. On my hands and knees, and face practically licking the floor, I examined every inch. Nothing. So, I jumped back onto my feet and pushed the chair toward the other direction. Again, I threw my body onto the floor and ran my hands over the wood-like tiles. My face touching the floor now, I side-eyed the floor from the same level.

Suddenly, I caught a shiny shimmer. No wonder the thing was tough to spot. Fortunately for me, a ray of light landed directly on it. Because the fake wood grains contained a mixture of grey, silver and cream in them, the sliver was somewhat camouflaged within them.

I whipped out my phone from my front pocket and opened up the camera. Quickly, I clicked seven separate photos, each from a different perspective and angle.

"You drop something?" my mother's voice crept up the back of my body, making me stand erect. I knew I looked plenty suspicious. "What on earth are you doing down there?"

It appeared she either forgot about the photo that Grams sent or maybe, just maybe, she never saw it on the plane in the first place. I kept praying that it was the second option. From the serious confused look on her face, it was obviously that.

How lucky was I!

"Sorry, Paulie. I thought I heard a coin drop from my pocket. But I guess I was wrong."

"Well, fix that chair. You don't want to upset your grandmother, do you? We are her guests, you know. It's bad enough that she switches around her furniture every other month. She's been doing that since I was a kid. Drove my father crazy!" my mother clutched my backpack and carryon then headed to the other bedroom down the hallway. I assumed she knew which one was mine.

Once Mom was gone, I continued my examination. But when I tried to pull the item free, I cut my middle finger on its edge. Blood already oozing, I stuck it between my lips and sucked on it to stop. The taste inside my mouth was metallic, like I'd licked iron. So awful. How was I going to be able to unwedge my assailant? I didn't want to be attacked again, and I didn't want to damage my Grams' new floors.

Then I realized that the area surrounding the tile boards had unusual gaps. Maybe I could find something to wiggle them slightly apart then lift it out. My feet flew into the kitchen, and I popped open the junk drawer. By a stroke of luck, there sat a Swiss Army knife with a thin blade tucked inside. Right next to it were a few loose Band-Aids. I grabbed one and opened it. Just as I finished wrapping my finger, my Grams reappeared. She took the empty paper from my hand and pulled open a cabinet in the kitchen's island. There sat a hidden trash basket. Grams dropped the paper inside before sliding the drawer away.

"Ah, I see you found it," her eyes sparkled with joy. "But beware. My daughter is on high alert right now. You're going to have to wait until nighttime to investigate more. I'll even help you."

With that, my grandmother repositioned the chair exactly as she wanted. Then she plopped all five feet two of her body into it, letting her short legs dangle from her white golf shorts over the edge of the cushion. Her feet barely brushed the floor. I decided to hop up onto the stool where my backpack once sat.

When Mom came out, she could surmise that the two of us were up to no good. We were silently grinning at each other, but Grams picked up on her suspicion and broke our silence.

"Not sure what you two want to do today after you wash up, but I was thinking maybe we'd head over to Siesta Key. That beach is special. The sand under your feet will feel like fine baby powder. So cool to the touch, too. Doesn't matter how high the thermostat rises. What do you say?"

My mother nodded approval and I went along with them both.

"Great. Now that that's settled, I can tell you it's a good thing because we're heading somewhere special tomorrow!" she went over to the package tucked behind the island from the post office and tossed it at me. It dropped to the floor but didn't clunk. The weight was light, and I was curious as to what was inside. "Go on," she coaxed me. "Open it!"

Her excitement spilled over as my mother merely rolled her eyes once again. I could tell she was in on it, whatever the surprise was. But at least, she wasn't frowning.

Once I pried open the flaps, I stuck my hands in and pulled out a paper with printed copy on it. At first, I was stumped. Nothing else appeared to be in the package, only this printed paper, an 8" by 11" folded. No wonder the box felt like a feather. When I unfolded it, there was a huge photo of a castle and labeled "Walt Disney World. Let the magic begin." Not noticing until now, there were three tickets, actually called Hopper Passes written across the bottom of their rectangular bodies. Each also said "Two Days."

"We're going to Disney World?" my body uncontrollably jumped up and down like a pogo stick. "We are? Really? Really?" my voice escalated to a high pitch. I hadn't realized it, but I was spinning around in a circle then fell from the dizziness. "When? When?"

"First thing, tomorrow morning. We'll get there bright and early and even eat breakfast in the park."

Instantaneously, my body flung itself at my poor grandmother, practically smothering her in her chair.

Paulie said, "That's right, Beans. Two days and two nights in Mickey's magic land."

Then she smiled at me with great satisfaction, "I think you're excited, right?"

Then I ran to my mom and gave her the biggest hug ever, "You know it." Then I pulled away and studied her smile. "You were in on this, weren't you?"

My mother didn't need to respond. Her face said it all.

Yet regardless of the exciting news of the famous mouse's house, my brain chewed on the thoughts of that silver sliver in the floor. I had to figure that out, but time was not on my side.

4

A PICTURE'S WORTH A
THOUSAND WORDS

The basement of Vito's house reeked of bacon. The generosity of Mrs. Rusamano filled my belly, and now I was sprawled out in Vito's beat up bean bag chair. Its burgundy rips and scars in random places now had gray duct tape seaming them together. The rough edges caught me by surprise, scratching against my neck. I thought about pulling my jacket on with its collar up just to protect my skin, but then I'd seem like a wuss. My eyelids struggled to stay open as my body began to slowly drift into a carbs-coma. That's what we called it. Anytime we stuffed ourselves silly with tons of carbohydrates, in this case – buttered toast, short stacks of silver dollar pancakes, yogurt and chocolate milk. The crispy slabs of bacon were a bonus.

While I groaned from overeating, Vito settled himself behind his computer, enhancing the photo from Beans' cell phone. This position meant we were in for serious business. Vito took command of investigations with critical concentration. With his basement set up like a professional laboratory with all the necessary bells and whistles, Vito prepared himself to tackle another investigation.

Only two bright lights broke through the darkness. Those circular arenas poured out from two high intensity gooseneck lamps. One was attached on an extended metal arm, fully screwed into position on the underside of the jam-packed cabinet shelves above the working countertop. Its twin was mobile, situated currently to the right of Vito's second computer screen, a traveling laptop, wide and bulky. Most of the white wood cabinets had glass encased windows. These allowed my friend to see his inventory at a glance. But Vito knew from memory where his equipment lived. In seconds, he'd locate even the tiniest push pin within a neighboring drawer or bin above and below. With the outside turning overcast and dark, no sunlight helped illuminate the area. Instead, it produced a calming environment that encouraged sleep.

"Tough to see much of anything with this one photo," my friend complained.

Vito was surrounded by the most sophisticated equipment ever. His personal forensics lab had been working overtime ever since Beans moved into Mill Creek. In only a short seven months, my new neighbor with the auburn hair and piercing green eyes delivered a mystery case for all of us to solve. At the beginning, I wasn't keen on any of it, tying up my time and distracting me from other things. Not that I had much to fill the void. But I would like to think that at least I had the option to do whatever my heart desired. Now, it seemed as though I was taken for granted – always being dragged into whatever new case she opened. Vito, too, was victimized. However, he seemed to be less worried about it. Her antics fell within a world that consumed him, too, so he approached it as work, not a hobby.

Gradually prying myself off the faux leather clump, I waltzed over behind him.

His red composition notebook lie open to his left. An ordinary white pen sat in its crease. The lined pages were blank on both left and right, but they sat at the ready for Vito's notes. I could see the writing on the pen. It was from Rivera's Pizzeria across the street. No doubt, one of his twin brothers Cesare or Dominick brought it home one night from work. They exchanged shifts and hours after school to make extra cash. I'd been here occasionally when they even came home with a free pizza in hand of which I'd managed to rob a slice. Other than the notebook, pen and computers, nothing else was poised for work.

What little I could see was a magnification of a jagged silver edge against a greyish black background. On closer look, the color was crisp and clean against the surrounding black, pale grey, and creamy ivory. I wasn't sure, but the photo had to be an enhancement of Beans' grandmother's phone camera work.

"What is all that?" I probed, unknowingly.

Vito grabbed a skinny black pen-like pointer.

"Never saw one of these, have you?" he chuckled, low and rumbly. "It's called a stylus. People use them with certain cell phones for business. Call them a Blackberry."

"Huh," I uttered, really unimpressed.

To me a hard plastic black thingie that didn't have any ink in it was a dud, just a random piece of junk.

Vito used the item to point at the computer. He never used his finger. He warned me once that the oil on my fingertip could ruin the monitor's screen. I didn't understand how, but I went along with it. I did know that the price tags on all of Vito's equipment downstairs rang up a tall receipt, no doubt in the hundreds. Maybe even thousands. And although a lot of it came secondhand from our local police station, maybe even fire department, I knew Vito paid for most of the devices and stationery and valued everything's longevity. He was about saving a buck and making investments last. After all, Vito intended to study forensic science in college while playing football on a scholarship. None of that happened yet, but it was a well-planned part of his dream. As a sophomore in high school, he had his head on straight and his eye on the future. His school schedule filled itself with mostly Advanced Placement courses in United States History, Biology, Trigonometry and English Literature. The majority of my other buddies and Vito's were goofballs who had no vision beyond tomorrow. They worried only about what kind of food was landing in their stomachs from time to time.

"See this here," the stylus traced a jagged line from left to right. "This edging is bumpy along here but from wear and tear. There's no longer a curved side. That's from extreme usage."

"Uh huh."

The mumbling that came next fell upon my perked ears like a birddog on a hunt. From the depth of a closet behind the stairs, I heard the heat kick on. The old furnace bellowed a growl and a creak. If I'd been a child playing down here, I'd be frightened to death of the basement monster.

"I can't tell much, like I said," he continued. "But my educated guess? This is a coin."

"You don't say. Like a dime or quarter, you mean?"

"Exactly. But not really."

"What's that supposed to mean?" my brain was clicking along and trying to follow, but it couldn't cope. "That's not a very clear answer if you ask me."

Standing up then digging into his sweatpants' pocket, my buddy pushed his hand in and pulled out a few coins. Along with them came some black fuzzy lint. He plucked out the soft furry bits and tossed them onto the basement floor. They made no sound when they reached the concrete.

"Here's a nickel, dime and quarter," he slapped them onto the white countertop near his computer. With his eyes at counter level, he examined their edges. "Come here. Look at these with me. What do you see? Look good and hard at them all. What makes them the same but what makes them different?"

Feeling like a dunce because I was no genius like my friend in the world of forensic science, I was wary of what to say after I studied them all. I even dared to touch them and turn them on the counter for extra measure. I didn't want to miss anything. Vito didn't taunt me often, but he got a kick out of teasing or tormenting me when I got something so obvious, all wrong.

From what I could tell, they had either smooth or rough surfaces. The quarter which seemed the oldest in circulation or maybe just overused, was dull and dirty, almost black in areas. The edge was curved, of course, like a circle would be but there were lines or ridges slightly carved into its side. The dime, although much smaller in size and lighter in weight, was extremely shiny and contained the same edging. Newer, too, I could feel the ridges as I slid my index finger along its round body. As for the nickel, the surface surrounding it was perfectly smooth to the touch.

I shared all those observations with Vito whose head nodded in agreement. His dark brown eyes studied mine when he acknowledged my accuracy.

"Correct," he said while I beamed, thrilled at my successful evaluation. "Now check this out." With a few flicks of his finger on the mouse and a click or two on the screen, his monitor offered three more images. Each one along with Beans' photo took up one quarter of the screen. All equally centered in a square space. I realized at that moment that I was looking at the three coins on the countertop. Now their images were zoomed in, increasing their details. This made it easier to make comparisons among all four pictures. For sure, the unidentified item in Beans' grandmother's photograph was not a match. Not even close.

I took a shot at my analysis, "Sure resembles a coin, just not one from our country."

"Bingo!" my man erupted. "You're on my wavelength. This looks like a coin but a far cry from our currency." Vito offered a little more, "Not even fashioned like one of our half dollars or silver dollars."

"So, what is it then?" I spoke. "I mean, where is it from?"

"Great question," he said, taking the black stylus and scratching behind his ear with it. "I can't tell much from this picture. I need more detail."

"How?"

"I have the perfect thing for the job," he stated with conviction, his hands now popping open a cabinet by his left leg. "This."

In truth, the small pewter box was an unrecognizable piece of equipment to me. It resembled another ordinary digital camera, one that I'd seen Vito use before. The only difference was the flatter surface, squared body, and tiny handles on its right and left sides. Also, there seemed to be special shutters on it from all four sides. They reminded me of ones that surrounded outdoor windows on a house or, could it be, a prototype of a drone? I was stumped as to what it was if it wasn't, indeed, a camera.

"This baby can take 3D images."

"It can do what?"

With that, the shaggy black hair of my friend whipped around, and he focused once again on his computer screen. With a few more strokes and bustling around, Vito called up a new bundle of images.

"Check these out," his computer screen lit up with an ordinary photo of the concrete wall behind Peyton Manning. The football quarterback's cardboard cutout stood quietly still in the back corner behind the beanbag seat where I'd rested minutes ago. Vito's dad, Chief Rusamano, purchased Peyton at the Columbus Market flea market off Route 206. The cut-out was lifelike in its Colts uniform, 6' 5" and worn from age and watermarks. But Peyton Manning's eyes pierced mine when I looked at him, a menacing stare of dedicated hurt. Those eyes always seemed to follow me wherever I wandered down here. "Last fall, I kept hearing a sound over there. At first, I thought it was outside – like a branch fallen from our elm tree, scraping against the plastic window well cover near the ground. But the wind wouldn't be doing that every day, all times of the day. I knew it had to be something else, and I never saw anything down here crawling around." His explanation began to give me the willies, thinking there might be a mouse or even a large rat roaming around, keeping us company. "I had only just acquired this puppy," he held up the machinery, "and remembered I hadn't broken it in yet. Fortunately, the fire department was going to swap it out for newer versions, and when my dad heard that, he knew I'd want to buy it instead. Cost a pretty penny. Five hundred smackeroos."

"Holy crap!" I said. I barely had that much in my own savings account. "That's a lot of dough."

"You're telling me, and the thing was used, no less," Vito swept his hair off his forehead then scratched the top of his head. "But see what it discovered."

The following images were both stills and short recorded video clips.

"This is inside the concrete. It got trapped somehow and kept roaming back and forth, trying to find its escape route."

Immediately, my pupils locked in on an image of a baby squirrel, struggling to find its way, a route to the outside. But it couldn't and it was panicking, starting and screeching to a halt, twitching in one direction then the other.

"See how this machine can first delve magically through the material, in this case – concrete cinder blocks, and pop up as a moving red box. The sensor targets the object then keeps following it, searching the area for movement or stoppage. Once I knew what it was, I felt sorry for the poor thing – trapped like that – and decided to come to its aid."

"Superman to the rescue," my laugh came out like a snort.

Vito mirrored my laughter, "Something like that." Then he shuffled over to the corner and pointed to the window at ground level. "See up there?" He tried to reach up far enough to touch it but couldn't. Even at five feet ten, Vito's fingertips were coming up short. "Just to the left of that spot, there was an eroded area in the landscaping dirt and mulch. It lined up with a seam of rotted mortar between the cinder blocks."

"No kidding?"

"And I can only think that the critter was in search of a nut or food that it'd seen or maybe smelled. But when it got too close, it either fell in or somehow got disoriented. After that, it was entombed in concrete walls."

Ironically, my brain suddenly flashed to a short story we'd just read in English class at school. Edgar Allan Poe's "The Cask of Amontillado." Some dude got revenge on a so-called friend by getting him drunk and encasing him while alive within a wall of the catacombs. Rest in peace.

"So, how did you set him free?" my curiosity was at its max. I couldn't imagine.

"I grabbed one of my dad's skinny dowel rods from his woodworking shop over there," he pointed again, this time to the other side of the basement beyond the steps. "Then I put some peanut butter on it and stuck that sucker into the crack." His eyes twinkled with glee, reminding me of the descriptions of Santa Claus in the "'Twas the Night Before Christmas" story. *His eyes, how they twinkled. His dimples, how merry.* Vito didn't have dimples, but the dude knew how to flash his eyes with joy when he was onto something or into something. This was that typical scenario. "Once the little guy gripped the stick with his teeth, I did a quick yank – like a fish on a hook – and out he popped. Actually," he started to laugh uncontrollably as he remembered the moment, "that sucker flew through the air and landed about twenty feet beyond that sturdy elm."

Doubled over from recalling the flying squirrel's release, Vito barely could walk back to his rolling chair.

My eyes seemed to cross as I pondered all of this, "So, why is this camera important right this minute?"

"My plan," Vito readjusted his body on the chair then his index finger tapped his temple, "is to overnight this baby to Beans. She'll have it by 8AM tomorrow morning. That way, she can take several images with it where that silver coin is and upload it to her computer then email them to me. Then voila! We'll know more with clearer data, actual dimensions, and everything. Who knows? Maybe there's not just one coin there."

"If it IS a coin. Hmmmmm," was all I could muster. My quarterback friend lived in a world unlike my own when it came to all this stuff. "Sounds like a plan."

"Do me a favor?" his forehead wrinkled up as he spoke. "Get her on the phone."

"Now?"

"Sure, now."

"I mean, right this minute?"

"Yes, there's no time sooner than the present," he smirked. "We need to get to the bottom of this. Besides, I've got nothing else on my personal agenda today. Do you?"

I shrugged, "Not really."

As Vito slid his seat over to the opened composition book and began to write, I punched a quick text to Beans.

You free for a quick call?

Without hesitation, I heard back.

Want me to call you? Or you calling me?

I pressed the FaceTime icon on her phone number and waited. Instantaneously, Beans' face appeared on my phone screen.

"Hey!" her voice was cheerful and high pitched with excitement.

"Hey yourself," I said. "Vito wanted me to call you."

"No kidding?" Bean's freckled face grinned. "What's going on? Where are you?"

"Down the basement."

"Hey, Beans," Vito spun around and tossed a wave at the phone as I turned it around for her to see. "We're going over that photo and . . ."

"And what did you find out?"

"Not much," Vito started. I was beginning to feel like odd man out, holding the phone between the two of them. That's when I decided to hand the phone over to my friend. "That's why we're calling. I need more data."

Beans shifted her position and suddenly we both could see that she was wearing a one-piece shamrock green bathing suit and was sitting in the shade of a beach umbrella. We could hear her mother's voice in the background and other noises. Some squawks and squeaks. Most likely, they were seagulls and kids playing nearby.

"Where the heck are you?" I asked.

"On a beach near Grams' house. Siesta Key, they call it. It's gorgeous," her prattling began to accelerate. Typical Beans. Getting all wound up and off the subject. "The sand feels powdery soft. They say it's because the white sand is actually made up of finely ground quartz – well, ninety-nine percent of it. And get this, it stays cool to the touch even in the hottest sun and temperatures." Her phone now was spinning around, turning this way and that, so we could take in the scenery around her. Both Mrs. Fagioli and Bean's grandmother shot us waves as the camera stopped on them. They, too, were in beach chairs but wearing lacy cover-ups of beige and white with floppy straw hats on their heads. In their hands were blue cans of Tocobaga Red Ale. I assumed they were cold beers. My favorite girl donned one of her baseball hats from the Pittsburgh Pirates, a gold cap with a black pirate logo above the brim. "It's already eighty-five here and it's only eleven o'clock. Bet it's freezing back home. Am I right?"

Both Vito and I slapped our heads and shook them. Beans was all drama and description all the time. I liked her so much, and even though she was a royal pain in my lower extremity, I found her fascinating and adventurous. Plus, even here in the animated FaceTime talk, she was bubbling over. So full of life. And cute as a button with her freckles darkening from the sunlight.

"Earth to Beans," Vito blurted out. "Focus, girl. Focus."

"I am focused," she said, not wanting to disappoint either of us. "Go on."

"I'm going to overnight you a piece of very expensive camera equipment. I'll send the easy steps to use it, too."

"Okay," she nodded and pulled the camera closer so that all we could see was the rounded orb on her shoulders. Only a few wisps of her auburn hair drifted onto her temples, blowing around a bit by the breeze there. "What am I doing with it?"

"More images," I now added into the conversation, not wanting to be left out. "This sucker," I delicately lifted the camera from off the counter and held it up for her to see, "takes three dimensional images. Moving and still."

"Wow! That's way cool," her voice sparkled with interest. "But you said you're going to ship it to me?"

"Yeah," Vito explained. "I'll overnight it to your grandmother's address. Fed Ex will deliver it by 8AM. I hope that's okay."

We noticed Bean's nose and mouth scrunch up a bit with concern.

"What is it?" I asked.

"Well, I'm glad to use it and get more information. I agree that we need it to figure out what we have here. But my Grams and mom surprised me with a mini-trip to Disney World. We're leaving tomorrow morning and not coming back until Thursday night." Her face was ever so serious now. "What if we leave before it gets here? It looks like a really valuable piece of equipment, Vito. I don't want to be responsible for something happening to it if we're not here." Her worried appearance was sincere. "It could be stolen!"

"Naw, don't worry," Vito said. "It'll be marked 'perishable food.' That will steer people away. What time do you leave tomorrow?"

"Not sure," she said. "But knowing Mom and Grams, it'll be early. I think the parks open at 9 o'clock. I forget, but I can check the brochures that Grams got for us."

"How far is it from your grandmother's place?" I asked.

We could hear Beans ask her grandmother then she came back to face us again.

"Just under two hours she said."

Vito chortled, "We heard!"

"Well, knowing my grandmother and mom, they're going to want to start early. Get their money's worth. You know what I mean?" my favorite girl now sounded worried instead of excited by the prospects of such a great trip.

"You're going to have to come up with a plan then . . . and stall them," I said.

"Yeah, stall them," Vito echoed.

Beans' face lit up, a complete turn-around. Knowing she had a challenge to overcome, her brain was already working overtime.

"Good luck," we both said, unplanned and simultaneously.

"I'll manage," she winked, and then she was gone.

"Whaddya think?" I said to Vito, taking my phone back from his hand then shoving it into my jeans pocket.

"I think our girl can do just about anything!"

And with that, Vito grabbed his pen and began drawing a chart on the virgin page.

He was right. Beans could do just about anything.

But it didn't sit right, what he said.

Beans was my girl. Or at least, one day soon she would be. I'd hoped to make her mine.

5

CLOSE CALLS AND GREAT ESCAPES

Sleeping was a major issue last night. The amount of fiery skin I had coating my body was enough to keep me tossing and turning all night long. Regardless of Paulie's numerous reminders to lather on suntan lotion and my constant applications, my delicate skin still took a beating. I blamed my mother's side of the family, half Irish with fair porcelain skin and blue eyes. Firenzi, her maiden name was her Italian father's, but Grams maiden name was O'Shea. Irish through and through. I had the blue eyes but mostly my complexion was like my own father's, the Italian Fagioli side. Olive skin tone tended to tan, not burn, but I suppose the intensity of the sun's rays closer to the equator could've been the reason for my unexpected sunburn. No blistering at least which was a blessing. Fortunately, I drank a lot of water last night, having to wake up and pee once around three o'clock. That was entirely unlike me. Then, to top it off, I was in a strange room and sleeping in a different bed, one that was much firmer than my sagging hammock-like mattress at home. Whatever the reason, my cell phone registered 6AM and I was wide awake yet foggy brained.

My bare feet hit the tile planks and were surprised to find a coolness beneath. I hit the toilet fast and detected the smell of fresh coffee brewing already. Out in the kitchen, I found my grandmother busying herself at the counter. She had a small red and white Igloo cooler sitting nearby as she removed slices of wheat bread from a sleeved loaf.

"Well, good morning, early bird," she chirped my way, joining the orchestration of other songbirds soaring through the screened in lanai. The air was crisp, not hot but just right. Comfortable even to my hot skin.

Grams was fully dressed. I could smell the suntan lotion already coating her arms that hung from her sleeveless peach-toned sundress. Surprisingly, for an older woman with a pale complexion, my grandmother had no signs of sunburn. Of course, she knew the secrets and system to beach time in Florida. I noticed that her toes dangled from a pair of Dollar Store flip-flops, bright orange, and her toenails were painted to match her lighter peach coverup. She was working on a menu of sorts to pack in the cooler. Her hips were swaying to the sounds from a nearby radio. The low volume was meant to keep us from waking up too early, I was guessing, and the music was unrecognizable.

"Oh, that," she pointed her butter knife at the plugged-in device. It had a volume knob and a tuner on one end while the other held the face of a small clock. "Local station around these parts. They play terrific salsa music." Grams put down the knife and crossed the short distance from kitchen sink to me. "Come here. Let me show you some moves. Watch my feet. Do what I do."

I had no option but to go with her.

My Grams delicately pulled me toward her by my waist. She took care not to hurt my stinging skin. Certain spots were aching more than others – like the tops of my shoulders and beneath my neck. I'm guessing I missed a few spots when I lathered on the Banana Boat 30 SPV. The fronts of my legs were a bright pink, too. But they only hurt if I touched them, and, of course, I couldn't help pressing the tip of my finger onto the redder patches, only to see a white spot appear then refill with red. A silly game that I played with myself, and I wondered if other sunburned teenagers did the same. I knew I was sunburned, but I had to keep testing and checking myself at the expense of a little pain. Masochistic, maybe.

When she slid her one hand behind my back, the touch was gentle and light. Her other hand clasped mine as she talked me through the steps and directions. All I had to do was move my right foot forward while she put her left one back. Then I reversed it. We did that a few times together before she released me, and we were freely moving to and fro, in sync. Grams was throwing her hips out as she moved back and forth, making the dance steps look sexy. Every so often, she tried to have me do the steps to the side and back, but I couldn't get the hang of that maneuver. The other way was simpler for me even though I occasionally tripped myself up, especially with my eight counts. But before I knew it, I was dancing some kind of crazy gyration with Grams. We were laughing our heads off, so loud that it woke up Paulie.

"What on earth are the two of you up to now?" her hands rubbed her eyes as she tugged down her Bruce Springsteen concert T-shirt.

Her nightwear was ratty and threadbare but comfortable. The shirt was one she bought with my father at a previous Bruce Springsteen concert. She wore it the night he died in a car crash at the hands of a drunk driver. The navy background was a pale blue now and the wording faded enough to have missing letters among the words – 2006 Tour. Seattle, Washington. Tour read "To" and Seattle now read "Seat." The state was unharmed, but still, the message "2006 To Seat Washington" was funny. Mom didn't care. It reminded her of my dad, and by now, erased the bad memory of his death and kept the happy memory of time shared together. They were so in love. I prayed I'd have that with someone someday. Naturally, my black-haired Adonis fit my picture of the future. But I doubted that Vito thought of me in that way.

"Your daughter has decent rhythm," Grams smiled as she stopped and encouraged me to take a bow with her. "We were taking a sandwich break to do a little Salsa," then she applauded for me to which I curtseyed.

Mom fought the mini-frown on her face in an attempt to show disapproval, but she couldn't help herself. Her body began to shimmy its shoulders and her fingers snapped to the music pouring out of the radio speakers. A sheepish grin snuck out from the corners of her mouth.

"Where on earth did you learn how to Salsa, Mom?" Paulie asked, reaching up to the cabinets in search of a coffee mug. "I didn't know you were into dancing. Well, at least not these fancy dances like those ballroom experts. You and Daddy always loved going to the Elks Lodge to 'cut a rug,' as you called it, once a month on Saturday nights. See. I remember." Her search continued, fumbling and clinking glassware. "You two did a mean jitterbug."

"Well, Miss Nosey-Rosie," Paulie's mother replied. "If you must know, I took lessons at our little clubhouse down the street. You know. I've mentioned it before. It's where I play cards with the ladies." Then the woman turned her head away as not to look into the eyes of her daughter. "Or Mahjong and board games. If you really must know, Mario took lessons with me."

With a job awaiting her, my grandmother's body danced its way back to the counter. Avoiding more grilling, Grams breezed by Paulie and took out a mug above the coffeemaker then spun its handle around in her hands to the beat of the music before handing it off to my mother. Then her head kept twitching before she continued layering out the slices, slathering them with mayo and mustard and piling on the ham, turkey, and Swiss cheese. We all liked lettuce so that was bunched on, too, but she kept the tomato slices in a separate container. I only liked them in the summertime. Otherwise, the off season, they tasted like nothing.

"Did you pack yet?" my mom stared me down. "And did you put on more aloe lotion yet?" Since her mother blew her off, Paulie was redirecting her frustration in my direction. "No need to overdo it. Just take the essentials for two days and two nights."

"Not yet."

"Not yet, what?"

"Not yet to either," I spoke, sheepishly. I had planned to do both last night but only took the time to relieve my burning skin. I figured I had plenty of time to pack this morning. I also was busy brewing a plan or two for the arrival of Vito's equipment. I had a few aces up my sleeves, but I knew that I'd be on the receiving end of wrath and anger, holding up departure time. "It won't take me long.

"Good to hear," Grams tossed us a look over her shoulder. "I'm hoping to get on the road no later than 8:30. There'll be a lighter amount of traffic even though it's a workday, but not too much. The parks open at 9 but we'll get there in time to have a brunch. I'm packing nuts and granola bars for the way to hold us over." Then she spied the sandwiches underway, "Oh these. We'll eat outside of the park for a break. Too expensive to do all the meals in there. Their prices are ridiculous, but most people pay them. Guess they budget for it."

"Either that, or they just are too lazy to plan on ways to save," my mother spoke brashly.

She had total disregard for people who were spendthrifts, wasting money without a care in the world when they had next to nothing to begin with.

As Grams worked, I studied the kitchen for the first time. I mean, really studied it. Grams had great taste in interior decorating. Her walls were coated in a combined pattern of black, mirrored silver, cream, and light gray tiles. They were staggered and rectangular in shape, fitted together in a delicate balance across the walls and under or between the pale gray cabinets. The countertops held flecks of cream, black and silver. I think she said they were granite. I didn't know much about décor so I figured I could look that up later. All the rounded and rectangular knobs were a satiny nickel color and the refrigerator, stove, microwave, and dishwasher all stainless steel. The kitchen was the epitome of modern, for sure. Then there was the tiny island in the middle of the room. Its location and size divided the area, and an extra sink sat inside it with a hook faucet that came on and off with a flick of the wrist or wave of the hand. Grams rinsed under it every so often. Magical maneuvering.

Paulie poured herself coffee and mentioned, ever so casually, "Hop to it, young lady. Or help your grandmother first then get a move on. And reapply more aloe gel to your sunburn. You hear me?" With that, my mom wheeled her body around and headed back to her bedroom. She took care in not jostling the mug to spill a drop of her coffee on

Grams' new floors. "You heard me, right?" she called back, muttering under her breath afterwards.

"Yes, ma'am."

"Not to worry, Quinn," my grandmother slid a drawer open by the stove and began wrapping the sandwiches in aluminum foil. "Why don't you check the fridge. Put fruit into bags. Just what you want. I'll eat anything, and I know your mom will, too."

When I opened the double doors, my eyes landed on freshly washed cherries in a light blue bowl. A few scrawny stems rested on the rim of the bowl, and I noticed a sort of spout on it for pouring presumably. Their color was deep and dark like a cherry cola. I couldn't resist popping one into my mouth. The flavor exploded on my tongue, all juicy and sweet. My teeth nibbled around the pit before spitting it into the sink. Grams laughed and admitted to doing the same thing, grabbing one from the bowl and imitating me. Suddenly, we were having a contest with how many we could push into our mouths and land hastily in the drainer cup. She won, but what did I expect. The woman had years of experience on me. I filled a baggy full to its brim and slid the plastic zipper across to lock in their freshness. Then I selected six plump mandarin oranges, Halo brand, along with a bunch of grapes. They, too, had a baggy of their own. Finally, three freshly scrubbed apples, red and luscious, joined their fruity friends.

"How about a few carrot and celery sticks?"

"Sure," Grams said as she playfully collided the bottom freezer door into my shin while reaching for three small ice packs. "I'm a sucker for rabbit food," she laughed. "Oh, and I have lemonade Snapple and water bottles in there, too. Can you get them for me?"

"No problem," I said, placing the fruit on the counter and tossing a carrot and two celery ribs next to them. My hands juggled the bottles before plopping them into the cooler. "That about it?"

"Just a couple more things," she added as she reached in the cabinet above the fridge. A bag of Hershey's kisses stood upright in a tin box along with two Cadbury chocolate bars. "For extra measure," her voice emitted a giggle accompanied by another mischievous wink, and she plopped them on top of everything else.

I thought I'd better share in confidence Vito's anticipated package.

"Don't worry about a thing, dear," the seventy-something woman's eyes searched around the corner of the hallway. "I'm sworn to secrecy. We'll work it out."

My grandmother was the best. She was my sidekick, my best friend, my confidante, and my Grams, not necessarily in that order. But the great part about Grandma Firenzi was how she always had my back and always was ready to listen. Naturally, there were times when she wanted to know too much, especially about my interest in Vito. But she could read between the lines. The sweet woman encouraged me and said that heartache can't happen if you don't let love in. Good point. Life was about risks. I certainly had learned that at the ripe old age of thirteen.

Once back in my guest bedroom, I wasn't sure what all to take so I put together an assortment of clothes. Two pairs of shorts, a pair of lounge pants – ultra-pink pajama bottoms but they could pass for casual pants, a handful of random T-shirts with crazy sayings on them from Columbus Market. They were a bargain at three for ten bucks. My favorite among them was the one that read, "I didn't fall. I attacked the floor." Because it was white with mauve lettering, it could go with anything. Another favorite was, "I'm not bossy. I just have better ideas!" Then I tucked in my white sneakers, a bunch of low ankle socks, a zip up navy hoodie and sweatpants. As I stared at my little duffle bag, one that we brought along with us for no reason until I now knew why, I kept wondering what I was forgetting. Did I need a bathing suit? My rinsed out one was hanging on the lanai. My grandmother's makeshift rope clothesline. I found myself smiling at my trip bag, thinking how funny it was to pack a smaller version of my stuff from what I'd already packed and brought in my carryon. It seemed so silly.

When I checked my cell phone, it read 8:05.

Paulie followed me out to the screened in porch, "We about ready?"

"Yup," I said, still curious what I was forgetting. "Just grabbing my suit."

"Oh, good idea," she gasped. "I forgot that they have heated pools where we're staying."

"They do?" my excitement bubbled over. I loved pools, indoors and out. "Where ARE we staying, anyway?" I asked, unaware of any details for this trip. My swimsuit was damp when I tugged it off the line then I took down my mother's. "Is it on property? I was reading that they have reasonably priced hotels there and you can use their transportation system to all the parks."

Mom took her suit from my hands, "If I remember correctly, your grandmother said it's inside the lands owned and operated by Walt Disney World, like you said. I think it's called Disney All Star Movies."

I was up late last night even though I was tired, reading up on all the parks and the surrounding hotels. My typical sleuthing mind wanted answers to so many questions. The popular family-oriented resorts included All Star Movies, and it looked really cool. Lots of movie theme landscaping and décor, both outdoors and in the rooms or hotels themselves. I loved the movies, and I knew that *Toy Story* with Woody and Buzz Lightyear were on the campus layout. Plus, the sorcerer Mickey from *Fantasia* and a couple of *101 Dalmations* dogs. For the life of me, I couldn't remember their character names. I never checked out the inside of the rooms, but I'm sure they tied into the movies well enough.

"Sounds fabulous," I said. "Hey, Mom. I think I forgot to bring underwear from home."

Paulie's eyebrows lifted in disbelief.

"Honest. I didn't pack any that I remember, and I just thought of that now. That's the one item I haven't packed yet."

"You sure you didn't throw them into the wash last night?"

"All of my underwear and two bras?" I mentioned. "Don't think so. That wouldn't make any sense."

"True, but we were all overtired yesterday - - from flying in then taking in the sun on the beach all day. Takes a lot out of you and can exhaust your brain. I'll check."

Then off Mom went with a shrug and a sigh.

I made my break for the front door. Ever so cautiously, I unlocked the dead bolt then the doorknob lock. The door squeaked open, and on the other side was Grams. It scared the bejeebers out of me.

"Grams!"

Her face contorted into laughter, "Looking for this?" She held up a small white flat box, no bigger than a cake box mix but about two inches deep. Barely any depth at all which meant the camera inside was flat, too. She hastily shoved it toward me, "Get to it, girl. Time's a wasting. Your mother's already giving me grief about not leaving at 8 o'clock sharp."

"She's used to her taxi time schedules, I'm afraid," I complained to her. "Believe it or not, 8 is late for her. Mom's already on the road anywhere between 5AM and 7AM." Grams rolled her eyes at me and shrugged. "Look, I shouldn't be but ten minutes."

"That long?!"

"Well, sure. I have to follow Vito's instructions inside then probably upload the pictures of videos to my laptop before emailing them to him." My fingernails broke open the seal on one end of the box. Immediately, I regretted my actions, breaking my middle finger's nail. "Drat."

Grams took off toward her bedroom after saying, "You know, I was only kidding. Right?"

I hustled to the spot on the floor. Calculating the space beneath the chair, I didn't move it, realizing I could use the camera without doing so. Besides, if Paulie waltzed out, I'd have to improvise a reason for my being on the floor regardless. Scrunching my body down to the floor tiles, I figured out the best way to position the camera and began clicking away on the remote control that came with it. Vito indicated that he needed the camera to be exactly on top of different sections for various coverage. Easily, the camera slid across the tiles' surface where it hovered above the data being collected. Then with a double click, I heard the videorecorder kick in. Like a drone gliding flawlessly through the air, I maneuvered its body until the doorbell rang.

"Who is it?" Grams peeped and flew down the hall.

I could hear my mom rambling behind her.

"I can't imagine who it could be," my grandmother's voice was concerned and emphasized each word loudly, a signal that I needed to hide.

I left the device underneath the chair and contorted my limbs into a fetal position, managing to be fully covered by the chair in front of me. My heart pounded erratically, practically leaping out of my chest.

Grams gasped unexpectedly when she opened the door, "Mario! What are YOU doing here?" From around the back of the chair, I could see my mother peering at him. My eyeballs strained to catch a glimpse of the man that captured my grandmother's heart, but I could only see the edge of his profile outside the door. "We're about to head off on a little trip. Celebrating my girls being here, you know?"

Surprisingly, the lilt in the man's voice was a bit higher than I'd imagined. In a way, it reminded me of the Saturday morning cartoon character Shaggy from "Scooby Doo." He spoke with a slight accent, too, but I couldn't make out if it was a regional dialect or indigenous to the area here in Florida.

"I figured as much," Mario said. "Saw your trunk open and you loading your beach cooler. Where you headed?" Then he hesitated a moment. "Oh goodness, where are my manners?" He must've out-stretched his hand because Paulie was extending hers now. "I'm Mario. Live just over there," he indicated, his long index finger pointed to the exact house. The color was a pale peach with white shutters and copper roof tiles. "I'm a close friend of your mother here."

His voice suddenly shifted into a curious tone, one that seemed teasing yet annoying. I figured he was doing it purposely to get a rise out of my grandmother and it did as she exclaimed, "Oh, Mario. Cut it out now."

Since they didn't seem to be stopping anytime yet, I finished the videotape, snapped four more pictures then packed up the camera and headed to my bedroom. I had to navigate my body cautiously against the lanai's sliding doors, inched through the kitchen and rounded the hall corner. Once in my bedroom, I grabbed my laptop from the bureau top where I'd left it, opened it, and attached the cable from the camera unit.

"Beans," I heard my mom call to me. "Come out here a minute. We're about to go, but your grandmother and I want you to meet someone. Hurry up."

The computer seemed to be taking an eternity, so I left it at work before flying out to the front door.

Meeting Mario was a treat. He was a taller version of Vito, dark complexion, full head of jet-black hair and lean but muscular. On top his head was a backwards Bass Pro fishing cap, screaming lime green and two fishing hooks piercing its lid. His beefy arms stuck out of a sleeveless white T-shirt that hung over his knee length trunks. Red to match his flip-flops. There were smudges of dirt around his black moustache and cheeks, smeared with sweat no doubt from work in his yard.

"You sure are the spittin' image of your mama," his eyes twinkled like my Grams. "Good looking DNA in this bunch," he teased. "Listen, I don't want to hold you ladies up. I'll get going, just wanted to see if you needed any help." Then he started to step away before adding, "I'll keep an eye on the house while you're gone." He gave Grams a big wink. "Oh, by the way, that tile company van parked in front of your house last night around midnight. Stayed there about ten minutes then took off. You heard from them lately? They just finished your floor last week, right?"

My grandmother shook her head no and didn't think anything of it. Then Mario's long legs started their return trip home. He happily whistled a tune and threw a hand into the air with a final wave, not looking back at us.

"Isn't he a sweetheart?" Grams said, batting her eyes at him. I caught my mother's own eyes twirling in their sockets, and that made me crack up. "I told you he was. Always a gentleman and always a huge help. I don't know what I'd do without him." She sighed, almost pining for him to return. "He's so dreamy," her voice was that of a schoolgirl's with a huge crush.

"Oh brother," I heard my mother utter under her breath, "It was nice meeting you, Mario," she called off to him. "I appreciate you looking out for my mother. I know how grateful she is."

"It's easy to take care of someone who is so adorable," he blew a kiss at Grams then at us.

The man was a charmer.

Once Paulie and Grams finished up their chatter, my mother whooshed me back to my room to get me moving. She darted into her own bedroom while I unhooked all the equipment. Satisfied, I group texted Vito and Booger to let them know that I was emailing them my accomplished feat. That took seconds. I didn't want to be inconspicuous with my mother. She'd get nosey if I took too long so I rushed the process, not waiting to see if the email's attachments uploaded and went through. I'd hear back fast enough. But if they didn't go through, I'd hear about it, too, and there'd be nothing I could do about it.

Ten minutes later, at precisely 8:26AM, the three of us females rode in the Audi up Route 75 North. Grams had on the Salsa station while Paulie leaned her head against the passenger window to catch a short nap. As for me, I propped my head against my pillow by the corner of the seat and examined the brochures for the four parks again. My brain attempted to plan a strategy to attack each park, figuring we could take in the sights at each of them both days. My plan was to visit Animal Kingdom first, especially since it was expansive and the animals on the safari would be more alert in the early hours of daylight. Then we'd hop over to Epcot to visit the countries, more of an adult park. Next, we'd take in Hollywood Studios and finally land at Magic Kingdom, the park that was the farthest from our hotel but also the most adventurous in my opinion. There were plenty of attractions at all of them, and each one sounded more exciting than the next. Like a dream come true, I was going to be having a ball with every new escapade and try to forget about the mysterious silver sliver back at Grams' house.

My cell phone vibrated in my shorts pocket.

Vito.

Everything came through great! Get back to you later. Booger and I are checking things out after lunch. Both of us have chores to do. Lucky you. On vacation. Cya."

Pleased with my sneaky endeavors a short while ago, I happily wallowed in my sense of accomplishment. But now the thoughts of what Vito and Booger might find lingered in my head. I didn't want it to bog me down. I was trying to keep focused on fun times at Walt Disney World. But somehow, I knew that my heart would only be halfway invested in my park adventures.

The real adventure lie in wait beneath Grams' favorite armchair.

6

KEEP THE CHANGE

Vito gave me a couple of tasks to accomplish before we regrouped later. I knew he was waiting to hear back from Beans once the digital operation system arrived. That's what Vito called it. To me, a camera was a camera. Pure and simple, no matter what fancy gadgets came with it.

Strutting my confident self across the street, I noted Granger, my old babysitter, resting his bottom on the aluminum folding chair in front of Clark's Hardware. His body was so lean that it took up only half of the tan seat. That was the normal location for Granger during the warmer months, but for some reason, he was there, all bundled up in the sunshine with a folded newspaper in his lap. Granger spent a good deal of his time tackling Jumble puzzles and challenging cross-word ones. He thought Word Searches were lazy challenges, yet he would do them to keep his brain activated. "Young Balthazar," he'd say to me, "You got to keep your mind chugging along like a locomotive up a steep incline. It keeps your brain cells sharp and keeps you from losing your marbles." When he'd say that to me, I knew the reason why. His wife Josephine, a young ninety compared to Granger's ninety-one years, was living in a memory facility because of Alzheimer's disease. She showed early signs of memory loss only a few years ago and her condition sadly underwent a rapid decline. It broke my heart. Josephine and Granger both took care of Haddie and me in his big old Victorian house near Mill Creek Bridge, a few houses down from where I stood now.

Today Granger wore a plain gold Sherpa's hat on his head, the ties dangling around his black chin. Around his neck wrapped a matching gold scarf with black flecks. His winter coat was bulky and zipped up to his neck, the dark brown collar flipped up behind it. His dark fingers stuck out of gloves that were missing their finger sleeves. That way he could grasp his pen firmly along with his newspaper. Granger always used a pen when he attacked his puzzles, knowing that he wouldn't make mistakes. I found that quite remarkable. The black boots on his feet were meant for a foot or more of snow, but he liked how their bulkiness kept him warm. Aging metal clasps gripped the tongue in place against the arches of his feet. They were dated in style, but that never kept Granger from wearing such things. He wasn't up to date in styles, not trendy at all. But no one cared. Granger was one of the most brilliant and highly respected people in the town.

"Young Balthazar," his warm face greeted me as I stepped onto the sidewalk. I loved that he called me by my given name and not my nickname, the one I was trying to shake from my childhood. Only Vito and my running mates ignored Booger and called me either Balthazar or B-Man. "How are you this brisk winter's day?" He gently blew on his fingertips then stroked the white stubble on his chin. "You look like a lad on a mission, son. Am I right?"

A sharp wind caught me off guard, enough to pull my wool hat out and tug it over my shaggy brown mop. I was overdue for a haircut already and felt like I was just at the barber's the other day.

"Short list of things to do," I nodded, showing him the folded paper in my hand. The yellow legal pad from Vito's basement lab held my agenda. "Vito and I are working on a new case, so to speak."

His eyes looked toward the sky then shut hard as he shook his head back and forth.

"Hmmmm," he began to respond without opening them. "Let me take a wild guess. Our girl Beans is busying herself with a pressing new adventure in Sarasota while she's seeing her grandmother."

My feet scuffed the concrete sidewalk beneath me, avoiding his assumption. But he knew me as well as my dad did along with my Babcia. I couldn't hide anything from another one of them. It didn't matter that we weren't blood relatives. It didn't matter that I was white and he was black. I considered Granger my family because of spending so many younger years under his charge. I trusted and respected him so very much. His caretaking and love of us kids in the community made all of us feel that way. We could always count on him.

I confessed, "Yes, you hit the nail on the head. Her Grams is the one who got the ball rolling on this one. That DNA is strong between granddaughter and grandmother."

"You don't say," he used the pen's plunger and clicked it against his temple.

"Uh huh."

That was the extent of our conversation. Not much to share yet. After all, neither Vito nor I had any specific details on Beans' discovery. But that would change once the evidence came in through the computer. I figured it would arrive shortly, but I promised to return to Vito's after lunch. That gave me some time to clean my room and play *Chutes and Ladders* with Haddie, her new game obsession. That and *Operation* kept her intrigued when she wanted to be interactive. Otherwise, she'd create buildings out of a deck of cards, draw or crayon in coloring books, dress up in costumes from her trunk or watch cartoons on TV. Babcia told me that my sister started watching Bob Ross reruns on television, too. His show was called "The Joy of Painting," and Haddie tried to imitate his painting talents on canvases. "Let's paint happy little trees," my little sister would whisper in Ross' soft voice. When I'd looked him up on the Internet, I saw that he had died in the mid-1990's, but still, people could enjoy his oversized smile and wiry afro. Other than that and a random interest in chess, Haddie enjoyed simple pleasures.

The bell above the entrance rang as I walked into the hardware store. Its tinkling lighthearted welcoming alerted Andy to my arrival, and he stopped what he was doing at the cash register.

"Yo, Booger," he said as I winced. "What are you up to this winter hiatus?"

Of course, Andy knew I was off because his kids were, too. They were probably in the back of the store with his dad around the paint stand. Speaking of paint, Andy looked like he'd been busy with brushes and paints himself, wearing a full-on set of painter's overalls that covered his entire outfit beneath. The baseball cap on his head advertised the store, "Clark's Hardware. 50 years serving Mill Creek." From head to ankle, the fortyish year-old guy was donned in denim.

"Gonna sound like a weird question," I commenced, "But is there a way to take apart tiles without breaking them?"

Andy finished shutting the cash register drawer before scratching his head.

"You and your old man trying to redecorate? What gives?"

"Nothing like that," I said. "A friend of mine thinks she lost something between two floor tiles. They're long. Look like wooden planks. Almost perfect, exactly like a real floor."

From behind my back, I heard a low growl. A recognizable voice. One that made me shudder.

Mr. Law and Order. Officer Wallace. My nemesis.

When I turned my head, I caught a glimpse of his piercing dark eyes. The policeman was on duty in his blue uniform, the brim of his hat level with his eyebrows, and the crisp crease of his pantlegs appeared from the knees down under his heavy navy, wool overcoat.

"Find what you needed, Rocky?" the shop owner asked, indicating to me to move to the side which I did in a heartbeat. I didn't need any attitude from the local cop. He had it out for me, and I didn't want to give him a reason to hate me more than he already did. "Looks like you're doing some wood staining?" Andy's hands swept up the two-quart cans of dark walnut stain and used the black wand attached to the register to scan the prices. Then he reached beneath the counter for a flimsy brown paper bag, flicked it in the air to open it and pushed the cans inside. "That'll be eleven sixty-one," the man slid the bag over to Officer Wallace.

The customer grumbled, "Highway robbery!" Then he pushed open his overcoat to reach into his pants' pocket. He handed Mr. Clark a twenty. "I could get these cheaper at Home Depot," Wallace complained in a gruff tone.

"Yeah, but like everybody else around these parts, you're too lazy to drive that far out of town. We're talking six miles, right?" Andy's laugh was from the belly, deep and rumbly. "I save you gas, too, you know?"

I couldn't help myself. I laughed, too.

"What's so darned funny, boy?" he extended his hand for his change without looking at Andy. Instead, his eyes locked with mine then studied me up and down. "You think you're so special."

The contorted face on Mr. Clark showed confusion.

"Not doing a thing, sir," I respectfully bit my tongue.

"Oh, is that right? Then why are you asking Andy about breaking up floor tiles? You planning to burglarize a few houses around town?"

I broke into hysterical laughter this time. The man was ridiculous. And even though I knew I was ticking him off, my impulse to giggle uncontrollably overcame me.

Andy jumped in to run interference for me, "That's nuts. Booger just had a circumstantial question. Nothing big deal."

"Oh, really. Prying up tiles in the floor isn't a big deal?"

"Not really," I piped up. "It's my business, sir. Not yours. No offense," I couldn't help myself. I just had to pop off at him. "I mean no disrespect," I finished up.

Mr. Law and Order was taken aback. The cap on his head came off, revealing his receding hairline that he fingered delicately before lodging the covering back in place.

"This town IS my business, son," Rocky Wallace's tone became intimidating. "And the people in it ARE my business. YOU . . . ," he paused before stepping a foot closer to me, "ARE my business." His nose practically touched mine, and I could smell his stinky breath. "You understand what I'm saying, chief?"

When he finished punctuating his last sentence with his index finger poking my chest, I wanted to haul off and sock him in the gut.

The criminal haunting of my summer before last kept the policeman and me miles apart. During the summer of 2012, I'd made the mistake of hanging with Vito and his football buddies on the board-walk at Seaside Park. There at a game of chance, the boys lost about ten bucks each and while highly disgruntled, jumped the stand to steal a bunch of CDs. Then we all took off for the beach, only to be chased by the local cops. The guys unloaded the heist onto the sand, and I unwittingly grabbed them to toss them into a nearby steel garbage can. That's when a police officer grabbed me by the t-shirt and took me into custody The other guys got away. I was innocent. Well, practically in my thinking. The other kids were the guilty ones. And Vito's dad, Chief of Police Pete Rusamano, would've been beside himself if he knew his kid was involved in shoplifting so I never ratted anybody out. But Rocky Wallace whose pals on the force heard of my exploits now thought I was a resident criminal. It figured.

When I checked with Andy Clark, the middle-aged man shot me a sympathetic wince. He was as uncomfortable in the situation as I was, and instead of pursuing Wallace's comments, asked me, "Is there grout between the joints, Booger?"

We both purposefully ignored the policeman, a dual force.

"I think so," I pondered, "but I'm not one hundred per cent sure. I can get back to you on that. They might be those interlocking ones, but I don't think so. Otherwise, how would something get stuck in between them?"

Clark agreed, "Right. The floorboards might be settling, especially if they were just laid. The grout between them is usually decorative more than functional so it's possible that the grout didn't set up right. In that way, a thin item could get stuck or fall between two of them."

Our conversation lasted another ten minutes before Mr. Law and Order seemed satisfied enough to exit to the outside under the ringing bell. Having Andy Clark validate my questioning benefited me more than he could ever know.

When I left the hardware store, Granger was gone from his seat. His folding chair parked itself up against the side of the building where it always stood when unoccupied. A slow stream of automobiles crawled toward me, entering town from Mill Creek Bridge. When I crossed the street by the old green street clock, a noticeable black SUV hugged the curb two doors down from my house. Officer Wallace was keeping a look-out for me and my whereabouts. I knew it. To throw him off, I decided to pull a stall tactic and jump into Aunt Gracie's variety store here at the corner.

Daisy Duke and her two little girls held the door open for me as they piled out, several bags hoisted in their arms. Even the littlest toddler tried her best to grip a heavy brown bag, but it was a struggle for her to climb down the steps.

"Thanks so much," I said to them all. "Good manners."

I grabbed the toddler's bag until she finished climbing down the steps and safely landed on the sidewalk below. That's when she reached up to carry it once again.

The girls' young mother never spoke much to me or anyone else as far as I could tell. But her smile told me she was grateful for the comment. From what I can sense, every parent likes to hear that their kids are polite. It proves that their upbringing is working right. I know my dad always told me that. "Good to know my hard work is paying off," always tapping me on the back of my head when he'd say it. Daisy Duke might've been a young mom, but she worked hard to raise her two kids as a single parent. No one ever talked badly about her even though she sometimes dressed inappropriately, a little too risqué and sensual. She had the figure for it and was truly a knockout, but it bugged me that she did it, being a mom and all. Here it was a chilly winter day, and the thirty-year-old woman had on ripped up jeans, high heeled white boots, and a heavy midriff red sweater with quilted jacket wide open for all to see. Maybe she was making an effort to find a new man in her life, a father to her kids.

Vito's aunt was standing at the back of the store, her hands busily rearranging a basket of pens and pencils on the counter. It wasn't until I cleared my throat that she discovered my presence.

"Well, hey there, Balthazar," her voice was delightfully cheerful, sincere in her greeting. "What can I do for you today?"

Truthfully, I had no interest in making a purchase nor was I searching for anything. I wanted only to avoid additional interaction with Drew Wallace's father. How could Drew, Beans newest eighth grade buddy, and Drew's family be so nice when their dad was so cruel. I knew that Mrs. Wallace was a sweetheart from the couple of encounters I'd had with her at Shoprite and from my Dad's own opinion. She didn't deserve a husband like him. I could only think that Mrs. Wallace was a better influence on her kids than their father. Mr. Law and Order was harsh and ignorant, lacking the polish of good manners that even Daisy Duke's kids already possessed. Or possibly being an officer of the law made his ego too large, thereby treating everyone else like they were dirt under his feet.

"Just window shopping, so to speak," I lied to her. "A friend at school has a birthday coming up and I'm trying to get ideas. Maybe I'll just look at the cards. I still have plenty of time."

Aunt Gracie came around from behind her post and pointed at a few stands of merchandise and shelves in different aisles. Her apple dotted apron led the way, their round red bodies floating and bobbing in the air. As a store owner, Gracie was always helpful and patient with her customers. In fact, she didn't chase kids out of her store like most places. Instead, she welcomed them all, knowing their loose change could purchase items just as well as any adult's billfold. To top it off, Aunt Gracie was also generous beyond her means, handing out lollipops to all the kids, no matter what age, and other goodies throughout the holidays. Her blondish hair showed signs of a needed touch up, the dark roots parting her locks at the center of her head while they were shining under the florescent lights of the ceiling.

I spied at my cell phone. Twenty minutes slid by before I decided to leave, empty-handed. But my ruse worked. Wallace's patrol car vanished, but I checked out the windows at the front end of the store besides my street. Nope. No car, no cop. I was good to go.

My exit and return home was in record time.

But when I got through the door and waltzed through the downstairs rooms, I found no one there. Babcia left my breakfast on the table with foil over it. No note. Nothing from Haddie either, other than a new painting left drying on the refrigerator door. Four triangular people stood from left to right on the eleven by fourteen piece of white freezer paper. Each person was fully labeled. First, at the left was Babcia with her babushka tied around her neck and a mint green dress to her ankles. Pop was next. His body above the waist was an upside-down triangle, and his tiny belt barely held up his work pants of beige with butcher's blood on them. I stood next to him and was holding my sister's hand. I, too, had an upside-down triangular torso but, unlike my old man, my waist was thicker, and I had on running pants with white stripes on the black. Finally, Haddie was almost as tall as me and definitely taller than our grandmother. All of us were smiling, and Haddie held an orange balloon in her left hand since her right one was occupied by mine. A Halloween costume, her inventive Bananaman from last October, coated her body. I studied it a little while longer and noticed Satan, our black Standard Poodle, sleeping under a leafy tree in the background. Still hungry, I returned to my awaiting breakfast with a glass of cold milk, thinking my Babcia and Haddie were most likely over at the church where my grandmother met up with her friends for card games and Bingo. Made sense. Just because I was home for the week for our winter break didn't mean Babcia's schedule would change. Since Haddie was off, too, Babcia would've had to take her along.

I wolfed down the grub but still found myself hungry. In the kitchen, I rummaged through the cabinets until I settled on a box of Saltine crackers. Then I grabbed the butter from the refrigerator and slathered gobs of yellow goodness all over them. On a hunch, I tried to look up images of Spanish doubloons on my cellphone while I devoured an entire sleeve of the salty, buttery crackers. But the only thing that kept surfacing was the term "pieces of eight" and "Spanish dollar." I clicked onto one of the sites and read.

The Spanish dollar, also known as the pieces of eight, was worth eight Spanish reales.

Reales? What the heck was that?

I tool a minute to sidestep and look it up. Reales.

A unit of currency in Spain. Mid-14th century. Replaced by the peseta in 1868.

Hmmmm, I thought to myself. These were another name for the Spanish dollar or its pieces. When I read a little more of the description, I realized that the peseta was related to a peso. That word I had heard of before. But I had always thought it was a Mexican coin.

About one and a half inches in diameter, the coin was minted in the Spanish Empire following a monetary reform in 1497. The coin was a staple in the economy for many years.

Huh, I thought. That size seemed the same as our half dollar. Guaranteed, the doubloon was worth a ton of money by today's standards. At least a few hundred bucks, I was guessing. I kept on reading.

Businessmen, tradesmen, and local citizens used the Spanish dollar frequently. In fact, cutting money in those days was legal. So, if people needed to make change, they would cut the Spanish dollar into eight pieces or "pieces of eight." If someone needed to purchase an item for "two bits," they would offer two sections of the dollar or a quarter of a dollar. Other countries adopted the Spanish dollar and countermarked it for their own purposes. The United States dollar based its own currency on the Spanish dollar until the 1850s. At the time of the minting process, the Spanish dollar's value altered in accordance with its weight in silver.

That's crazy, I thought. The value changed according to how much silver was used in the minting process. Often then, a person could be getting paid more than less. It didn't make sense. That would be like today saying a pair of shoes were worth fifty bucks but instead of paying two twenties and a ten, it'd be like having two twenties stuck together to two other twenties and the ten doubled. Then the shoe shop would actually earn double or one hundred bucks, a big overage in payment. I wondered if anybody back then thought of it that way.

Then I found a different site that offered more clarity on weight.

Melted silver or gold was rolled out to a common thickness. When coins were cut and stamped, they were weighed. If the weight was inaccurate, the craftsman cut off enough from one edge then reweighed the coin. This is the reason why doubloons often are unique in shape and not fully round or circular.

Okay, I thought. Now that makes more sense. But I'm sure a few sellers or buyers got stiffed. How couldn't they?

I finished surfing the 'net for more information about reales, values, evidence in museums, and other stories, especially ones of ruthless pirates, their attacks, and their ends. The reading material was fascinating, and I wasn't one for reading all that much. If reading in school was as interesting, I wouldn't find my classes or teachers so boring.

My phone started singing, "I fought the law, and the law won. I fought the law, and the law won." The Bobby Fuller Four. I knew the group's sound well. After all, it was Vito's calling card, and he insisted I keep the song linked to his name.

"Hey ho, bro," his voice contradicted itself, sounding both tired and upbeat at the same time. "You want to come over now? I got done sooner than I'd expected."

I checked the clock on the stove. 1:10PM. Where had the time gone?

"Sure," I said. "Give me five."

"You got it."

Opening the junk drawer next to the refrigerator, I scrounged around for a piece of paper and a pen or pencil. No luck with either, but I did see a purple magic marker. It was the one that Haddie was missing from her crayon box in the toy chest between the dining room and family room. Aha. If anyone had paper, it would be Haddie. My feet shuffled over to the chest and inside I found a drawing tablet right at the top. I ripped out a page then wrote, "At Vito's. Be home by dinner. If you need me, call." Then I made Xs and Os for kisses and hugs since Haddie would be able to read them. At only seven, her reading skills were lagging behind her classmates. Her skill set for an autistic child had its peaks and valleys. While excellent in math and numbers, Haddie knew the alphabet and sounds but not too many reading words. Her special teacher at school was working on that so she was improving, but it was slow going.

Satisfied at leaving the note in the middle of the dining room table, I grabbed my coat, pulled on my knitted cap, and rushed off to Vito's basement. I couldn't wait to share what I discovered.

He'd be proud of me.

More importantly, Beans would be proud of me.

7

MAKING A SPLASH

Complaining wasn't my middle name. But the heels of my feet were aching from walking on the hard surface down Main Street, the official entranceway from the admission gates of Magic Kingdom. My grandmother and mother warned me to change into my sneakers in the car like they did, but I didn't pay any attention. My body was too hot, and I figured my toes being exposed in my flip-flops would keep me cool. Not the case. I was hot, regardless. Back home, it was warmer than normal, Drew told me. She texted me on our drive here. She said that it was in the mid-50s, relatively warm for the Northeast in February. The thermostat in Grams' car read 74 when we left her driveway. By the time we pulled into a designated parking space in the Goofy section where we rode the tram to the entrance, Grams' car thermostat read 86. In only a little more than an hour and a half, the heat intensified twelve degrees. Any which way I looked at it, I couldn't complain out loud to Paulie or Grams. They would only say, "We told you so."

When we'd arrived on Interstate 4 West that led to the parks, I suddenly had a change of heart. My plan flipped to hitting Magic Kingdom first, especially with all my road trip reading about the different fairytale rides, stories that made me nostalgic for my childhood.

Grams agreed that a day with "The Mouse," as she referred to him, would be a stellar way to start our mini-vacation. "There's so much more fun and excitement in Magic Kingdom, and we can hit all three parks easily tomorrow. Don't get me wrong. They offer all kinds of great things, but we can whiz through them. If time allows today, we can always try to squeeze another one in. And don't worry. I second your motion." My mom merely went along, knowing she'd be out-voted anyhow.

The walkway to Cinderella's castle, the huge building in the mid-dle of Magic Kingdom, was buzzing with families. Many of them intentionally dressed in duplicate outfits, maybe so they wouldn't lose one another in such an enormous place. That was my biggest fear. I didn't want to lose sight of my mom or grandmom, only because they carried my money and my snacks in their pocketbooks. I wasn't afraid to be stranded. There were far too many things to see and do. Instead, Grams and Paulie would be the ones to freak out. I used my map of the park and a pen to check off a few buildings that I wanted to revisit before we left at night. The candy shop called Main Street Confectionary took up one entire corner on Main Street. Caramel apples, cake pops, marshmallow wands, iced cookies, oversized swirl-ing rainbow-colored lollipops and yummy chocolates lined their dis-play windows, all coaxing their customers to empty their wallets inside. I knew I could buy a treat for the hotel when we left later and headed back for our sleepover. Just beyond that was another small building that looked like an outdated movie theatre from the 1920's. Inside were old fashioned machines that flickered black and white stories on cards like a Rolodex. When a nickel went into the machine's slot, the cards that were all hooked together flipped fast around a cylinder to make the people on them dance or jump or run. They were funny to watch. But since my Grams calculated a game plan for our route, we seemed to be on a hectic time schedule, fitting in what interested us. Even though Grams had a lot of knowledge about the parks, none of us including her had ever been here before so we had to make every single second count. Time, as they say, was of the essence.

Surprisingly, Paulie wanted to walk through the castle's arches, not around the mammoth building. The leading path rose up under our feet until we reached the magnificent opening at the top of the incline. Built to resemble actual castles that exist in Germany and France, the Cinderella Castle was nothing short of magnificent. Its spires and trimmings were a royal blue, sitting among and above the creamy tones of bricks speckling the walls. There was a drawbridge, but it didn't open or close. Instead, it suspended itself over a moat of three million gallons of water.

Once inside, we closely inspected the walls to both left and right of us.

"These murals are made of glass," Grams exclaimed, running her fingers over the face of their smooth surfaces. "And look," she spun around to study the opposite side, "the five scenes tell the story of Cinderella. That's so cool."

Her wording always made me giggle. Grams didn't try to be cool when she did this. It's just the way she was. Always was, Mom claimed.

My mom spotted a couple signs that indicated Cinderella's Royal Table.

"I think I read that that's a restaurant. You can make a reservation to eat in there," Paulie said. "Probably costs a pretty penny."

Being a spendthrift, only my mother would think about money and frugality at a time like this. She admittedly said we would "splurge a little" on this vacation, but we certainly wouldn't go overboard. Mom always saved and cut corners wherever we could. It made sense. She was the one and only bread winner in our household, using her self-employed taxi service to keep us fed and lodged. She exhibited her bargain hunting from the time I was little in Seattle, Washington, and when my dad died in a car crash, she continued more of the same once we moved in with Grams and Pops in Galveston, Texas, then in Steubenville, Ohio, and finally Mill Creek, New Jersey. Paulie confessed that Dad, on the other hand, was not a penny pincher. On the opposite end of the spectrum, he was a spender. Nothing overboard, but he didn't worry about taking us out to restaurants or hitting up the aquarium or rooting for the Mariners at their ballpark. It bugged Mom, and Dad forever teased her about it. I missed him, a man I truly never got to know. He'd love this new adventure with Grams, and I guarantee we'd already be sucking on one of those supersized lollipops as we walked.

We took a pitstop to ride *Prince Charming's Regal Carousel* on the other side of the castle. Paulie chose to sit on a green saddle. Her horse's white head turned to the right, its mouth open to bite at mine. My stallion's head was lifted up toward the sky as if to buck its hind legs and take off on a race. Grams straddled a blue seated steed all the way on the inside. Her giggles were lighthearted and fun loving. The three of us suddenly seemed like five-year-olds, riding a merry-go-round for the first time in our lives. While we circled around and around, I noticed other rides that I knew we had to tackle. *The Many Adventures of Winnie the Pooh, Peter Pan's Flight, The Mad Tea Party, Dumbo the Flying*

Elephant, and *It's a Small World.* Fortunately for me, both Grams and Paulie loved rides.

Both Winnie the Pooh and Peter Pan were what parks called Dark Rides, ones that you rode through with an inside story in a slightly illuminated space. The only sections brightened were the scenes in the stories about the stuffed honey bear in Hundred Acre Wood and flying boys from Neverland. By contrast, *Dumbo* reminded me of the helicopter rides at carnivals where the rider operated a joystick to go up and down in the air. Only with *Dumbo,* we rode in a mini-version of the baby elephant. Grams got a little queasy on *The Mad Tea Party.* I supposed I was a little too heavy handed on the spinning wheel that controlled our cup. Paulie found it hysterical, laughing so hard that she was coughing and, initially, couldn't catch her breath. Tears were running down her cheeks from such uncontrollable laughter. Plus, I think seeing her mother woozy, made my mother laugh even harder. Once we climbed out and walked through the exit gate, Grams had to find a bench to hang her head between her legs in case she threw up.

Paulie grabbed a bottle of water from her backpack and poured a little in her cupped hand for Grams to drink. Then she poured a little more and patted the back of my grandmother's neck to cool her down a bit. Guilt seemed to be setting in, replacing my mother's laugh fest.

"Thanks, honey," she barely could speak. "I'm feeling a bit better. Guess I'm getting a little too old for spinny rides," then Grams laughed ever so softly followed by a long groan.

About ten minutes later, we were on our way again when my grandmother was no longer green around the gills.

Looping back toward the castle, I noticed a most colorful house. Its expanse covered the width of about four buildings, and the face of it, including its roof, was multicolored with pink, gold, red and blue. Waving fifty to seventy-five feet above us were little flags in well designated, purposeful positions. Above the entrance door was a banner that read, "Welcome to the happiest cruise that ever sailed." Floating heads of children around the world rested upon half-bodies that sat in a boat together, luring us visitors indoors.

Grams led the way, "I've heard of this ride before. If I recall correctly, it was featured first as a Walt Disney creation at the New York Fair in 1964 and 1965. I think Pepsi sponsored it." Grams continued to explain the ride's history. She loved history. So did my mom. From solving mystery cases, I was beginning to develop an interest in it more myself. "Walt Disney's creators wanted to originate a ride that encouraged peace around the world, especially after the wars that engaged our country. World War I, World War II, the Korean War. His fear was that America would enter the war that was already looming in Vietnam. Little did he know that five years later in 1969, we would have soldiers there. Senseless deaths." The older woman shook her head and sighed. "But this ride was about peace. Peace among the world. Peace between countries. It's got a lovely message." Then the old woman sighed, "And the fact that it's delivered by children makes it even more precious. After all, they are the future. YOU, dear, are our future," she reached for my hand and squeezed it tightly with even more reassurance.

"You never cease to amaze me, Grams," I told her, hanging on and digesting every word.

Just before we entered, Paulie announced her call to nature. Luckily, there was a restroom sign nearby. Easily recognizable, its stick figured man and woman in basic blue pointed her in the right direction.

"I won't be long," she yelled as she jogged off, crossing the walkway, and dodging a few people who were in her way.

Grams found a bench to park on while I decided to check in with Booger. Her eyes slightly closed once she slid into the shade of an old oak. My assumption was she was catching a few winks to rejuvenate herself. Or maybe her tummy still was unsettled from the *The Mad Tea Party*, but she didn't want anyone to know or worry about it. After all, my Grams was sixty years older than my thirteen years.

My own body had a hard time getting up. My sweaty thighs sticking out of my white shorts pried themselves free from the wooden bench.

"Hey there," I announced myself to Booger when he answered his phone, and I began to pace around, keeping an eye peeled for Mom's return.

"Saved by the bell," he mumbled.

"Whaddya mean?"

"Just ran into our mutual enemy a little while ago," my neighbor exhaled loudly into my ear. "He sure is a busy body, always trying to stick his nose into my business. Actually, YOUR business that I get sucked into," he emphasized the *your* to make sure I understood his underlying message.

I felt awful for him. I knew how much he tried to avoid Officer Wallace. I had asked Drew, his daughter who was my fair-weather friend in my 8th grade class, why her father had it in for Booger. All she could say was, "When my dad makes his mind up that he doesn't like someone, it doesn't matter how old they are or what they do, he digs his heels in and makes their lives miserable. It's just his way." I disagreed with that behavior. I spoke up and let her know that since she liked Booger, she should work on her dad to come around and give the boy a break. Who knew if she tried or not? I didn't want to dwell on it.

"So, where'd you run into him? Or did he run into you?"

"I was over at Andy Clark's about an hour ago. I'm home now, thank goodness." Then I could hear him munching away and whispering to someone. "Sorry, eating a late lunch. Don't mean to be rude but I'm starved."

"Who are you talking to? Is Vito with you? You guys get any data from the pictures and video I sent out?" I was whispering now, not knowing if my Grams was actually drifting a little or if she was eavesdropping. Most likely the latter. "Whose there?"

"Just me, Babcia, Haddie and Satan. That's about it. And no, Vito and I haven't gone through everything yet. We're planning to do that at around 2 o'clock. He had some other stuff to do for his old man first then he told me to meet up again." His next bite must've been huge because I could barely make out what he was saying with his mouth full. My mother would not approve, always reminding me of the rule of not speaking with food in my mouth. "But I do know that we agree that the edge of that silver thing your Grams found resembles a coin of some sort."

I digested the words he said.

"Since he mentioned a foreign coin, something from a different country, I personally thought about doubloons. You know. Pirate booty."

"Really? Pirate booty. How in heaven did you come up that random idea?"

"Well, you're in Florida, right?" he began.

"Right," I had no idea where he was headed in this conversation. I started walking in the direction of the restroom, praying Paulie wouldn't be back too quickly. This talk was only beginning to become intriguing. But I was wrong. There I spotted her, leaving the ladies' room area, and strolling back towards us. "Be quick," I rushed, not meaning to be rude. "I've got to hang up in a few seconds."

"Okay Okay," he stumbled forward, vocally. "Well, New Jersey had plenty of shipwrecks up and down our coastline. People have been known to scavenge around with those metal detectors, sweeping over the sand. Lucky if they find a quarter here and there," his pace quickened. "Knowing that, I decided to look up Florida's history with shipwrecks and pirates. There've been plenty. On both east coast and west. In fact, an hour north of Sarasota, there are plenty of spots. So, I figured, maybe that silvery sliver is only the tip of the iceberg. A piece of pirate's booty with more nearby."

"You're crazy!" I snapped at him.

Paulie, not seeing me on the cell phone because my body was turned in profile to her, barked at me, "Are you calling ME crazy?"

"No," I put my hand up. "I gotta go. Later."

"Oh, I see," she said. "You were on the phone."

I tucked my phone away, "Yeah, checking in with Booger. Just filling him in on our trip so far. He says to have a great time."

But my mother knew better, and she gave me a hard look. Her eyes examined my expression and studied my fidgeting hands which always gave me away.

"We'll talk about it later," my mom bit her lip. "Let's get on that ride. Mom? You awake?"

My grandmother's eyelids lifted, and her mouth drew up into a wide grin, "I sure am." With that, she gave me a wink, meaning she heard every word of my phone call. "Let's enter that small world. I can't wait."

And with that, my grandmother's older body suddenly leapt up like a kid jumping from an airborne swing on a child's playground. Her gait sped off, leaving Mom and I in her dust.

Once inside, we joined a line, already formed, twisting and turning, and guiding us through switchback queues. They were roped off with steel stands. We serpentined our way to the front eventually, only about ten minutes wait time, and prepared to enter a big boat. One approached, all blue and wooden but it looked slick and shiny, like it was covered in oil. Packed full of adults and kids alike, we couldn't help but notice their expressions of complete satisfaction. Their smiles stretched across their faces, from ear to ear. Each water vessel had five rows and seemed to hold around twenty people.

Ours finally jerked forward after unloading its passengers. As luck would have it, we climbed into the front row. That would enable us to see every detail as we rode along. The Cast Member, apparently the name for the people who worked around the parks, led us onboard. She mentioned that the ride took about thirteen minutes, one of the longest entertainment rides in all Magic Kingdom. That was impressive. Normally, rides, especially the best roller coasters and dark rides, only lasted two to four minutes. "Look both to the right and to the left plus up and down as your boat moves along or you'll miss all kinds of details. And remember," she told us new passengers, "You're going to travel the world. You'll start on one continent and end on another. See if you can recognize all the countries that are represented," her voice trailed off as our boat lurched forward. Her body was clad in a short teal jacket, sky blue shorts, blue and white striped shirt, white stockings, and straw hat with matching teal ribbon. A chunky arm thrusting out of the teal jacket waved goodbye to us all. I couldn't see what she wore on her feet, but I imagined they were either wooden shoes or costume boots, another addition to her fairytale-like costume. People in the rows behind me blocked my view on my final glance. "Have fun!" she chirped enthusiastically, still waving with glee.

It was only then that I truly realized that I was in a magical fantasy land, the world of Walt Disney and his imagination. Magic Kingdom.

The brightness at the opening archway began to fade as we drifted along the waterway. While we floated through the murky water, the sky darkened. To the right, bright whites and silvers and blue hues welcomed us. The Cast Member was one hundred per cent correct. There was so much to view that my eyes felt like they were popping out of my head. At the get-go, doll-like children were singing, drowning out the previous greetings of "Bonjour, Hello, Jambo, Shalom, Aloha" until all dissipated. "I think that's Scandinavia," Grams whispered in my ear. She pointed at the ice skaters whirling around and singers in native dress. The kid figures dressed warmly against their icy backdrop. Not more than a minute later, we were entering England, Scotland and Ireland while leaving Denmark and France behind. In nanoseconds, our boat paralleled two universes, one in Northern and Middle Europe while dipping our toes into the United Kingdom.

How quick was our voyage, floating sleepily past multiple anima-tions. Above us dangled banners and birds and orchids or lilies. Flashes of spring colors turned to autumn or winter then back to summer, in no particular order. Palm trees sprouted up in unexpected places, resembling the types that lined Grams' street or rooted themselves in her front and back yards. All the while as our eyes darted all over the space, we heard children's voices singing merrily, "It's a world of laughter, a world of tears. It's a world of hopes and a world of fears. There's so much that we share that it's time we're aware, it's a small world after all. It's a small world after all. It's a small world after all. It's a small world after all. It's a small, small world." Transitioning from one country to another, the scenery not only changed but also the children's outfits and the lyrics in their own country's language. The whole thing was spectacular. I could think of no other word to better size up the experience.

Upon our exit, we realized the summarizing finale. Voices excitedly exclaimed, "Sayonara, Adios, Ciao, Au Revoir, Goodbye" while the doll representatives from all around the world celebrated peace and tranquility with dances and games and gestures. Lingering in the background was the theme song.

"I think India was my favorite with its Taj Mahal and flying carpets," Mom shared with the two of us as we headed to the dock, "and the giraffes and monkeys plus all those brightly colored, different flowers in Africa."

Grams didn't hesitate to call out her favorites next, "Me, I loved the Rain Forest and the Hawaiian Hula dancers and the roller coaster at the end and how all the children were mixed together, playing, having fun while we were leaving."

Our boat suddenly bumped the one in front of us. A four-year-old girl behind us with yellow pigtails let out an "Eek" immediately followed by, "That was fun, Mommy. Can we do it again?" Her mother hushed her then lifted her up and placed her feet, covered in pink

Mickey Mouse sneakers, onto the platform. We waited until everyone cleared before climbing out ourselves.

"You didn't mention *your* favorite part?" both my mother and grandmother said together. Then they locked pinkies and said, "Make a wish." Closing their eyes like young children would, the two special women in my life took a moment then stared at me once more.

Truthfully, I had no favorite. I found the entire ride mesmerizing and educational. But I knew they wanted me to say something specific.

"I guess," I started, "if I have to choose, it'd be the flying carpets and the roller coaster at the end." I was smart enough to know that I had to play the diplomat, choosing what both my mom and Grams liked. It kept me safe but honest. They were, indeed, two of my favorites, but so were about a gazillion other things. "Actually, I loved the whole ride," I explained. "I found it breathtakingly beautiful."

Together, my mom and grandmother exchanged looks of satisfaction then nodded.

"If no one has an objection," I declared, "I'd like to go on that pirate ride." The thought of pirate booty floated in my brain after Booger's call. He'd planted the seed, now I wanted it to germinate. "It's not far from here," my fingers grabbed my grandmother's hand and whisked her almost out of her sandals.

"Hold your horses, girl," she laughed. "The ride's not going anywhere. And, by the way, it's called *Pirates of the Caribbean*. Like the movies that came out after it. We watched the first one together, remember? You were only around nine then when we watched it. You and your mom were living with your Grandpop and me in Galveston." Her feet hastily kept up with mine. "On that island, you became obsessed with pirates."

My memory barely recollected that. I was only a kid then, but I do know that I still hold a special spot for pirates in my heart. A fascination, as it were. I always felt sorry for them. As if none of them had any talents but to navigate the oceans and waterways on their ships and looted trade routes for a living. I always figured they didn't know how to do anything else. And most of them didn't have a family, just each other. I suppose they were each other's family, but I'm not sure they could trust one another, what with all the thieving and stealing and all. They were like a modern-day mafia, always looking over their shoulders because they feared for their own lives while threatening the safety and security of others.

Grams unfolded more details, about how Paulie searched for sand dollars on the beach while I searched for buried treasure. Grams said I always told her that one day we'd all be rich when I found their hidden treasure chests, all washed up on shore from their destroyed ships. True, many shipwrecks happened up and down the east coasts where immense boat loads of cargo dove to the bottom of the sea. The Atlantic Ocean side of the country had its lion's share, but other sections of the United States held many, too, in the deep. I knew very little about it, but I was willing to dig in deeper, especially on the Gulf Coast where Grams now lived.

Pirates of the Caribbean was one of the most popular dark rides in the Magic Kingdom. The long lines outside its entrance proved it. Sadly, I had misjudged my map skills. The distance between Adventureland and Fantasyland was farther than I'd anticipated. But on the upside, I convinced my mother and grandmother to stop and buy a turkey leg for us to share on the walk. A whole Thanksgiving sized turkey leg, all crispy on the outside, and moist and juicy on the inside. Who sells just a turkey leg for a snack? I thought. Why Walt Disney World, of course. The place where magical dreams come true. It made me giggle as we passed that leg among us.

My napkin swiped off the grease from my lips when my phone vibrated in my pocket. When I lifted it out to check it, I spotted a text from Vito. My black-haired Adonis.

Heard you're at the Magic Kingdom. Sweet!

Thanks. I quickly responded, lagging a couple steps behind my Grams as they swapped the turkey leg back and forth. My heart was speeding up at the thought of him. *What's up?*

If you get a chance, ride Pirates of the Caribbean. Look for doubloons. Take pix. Send to me. I hear they're in a special scene and relatively authentic.

What a lark. What timing.

Just arrived. Such a coincidence. Will do. Later.

Over and out.

His last message followed with a happy face emoji and a thumbs up. And my heart skipped a beat.

Interestingly enough, when I'd done my millionaire project on Walt Disney last month, I discovered that Mr. Disney was a stickler for details. He wanted facts and exact duplications to be as authentic and realistic as possible. The likelihood of doubloons showing up within the dark ride could prove helpful to our new case. What appeared in the scenes inside would benefit us in the long run, I hoped. On top of that, my boyfriend-of-the-future would admire my findings. Scoring a point for more attention from him, perhaps. At least, that was a distinct possibility. I wanted desperately to be his girlfriend. Not that I ever really wanted a boyfriend before. I wasn't desperate like my friend Drew Wallace who longed to be Booger's girlfriend. I knew my neighbor had no interest in her, but I encouraged him nonetheless to at least give her a little attention. Maybe, such a romantic partnership might get the heat off my friend from Drew's dad.

Checking her watch after answering a phone call herself, Paulie informed us that she was starving and heading to Grams' car to retrieve our sandwiches. I couldn't argue with her. The turkey leg, while delicious and timely, didn't fill me up either. Merely an appetizer. Grams agreed to go on the ride with me, curious to see what storyline would prevail this time around. She loved how everything in this magical land had a story of its own so far.

A black sail hooked onto the mast of a ship's face greeted us near the entrance. Already, I loved this ride, duplicating a ship wrecked on the coast. Inside the building, we seemed to be walking beneath a building – seeing its pillars and load bearing cross beams plus arches. Twilight or dusk was the hour, yet the sun shone brightly only fifty feet away outdoors. The stretched walkway became less and less visible in the darkness with torches leading our way. Only a handful of families walked before us, making the trip to the loading station a quick one. Our boat was similar to the one at *It's a Small World*, just not colorful – merely plain wooden hulls. Again, unlike our last attraction, the caverns were full of shadows and dark colors. Navy and browns and blacks and grays. A sandy beach lined with skeletons, one with a sword in its back, made an initial greeting. An apparent warning to us visitors who dared to cross paths with the wildly fierce pirate bands. Glaring white eyes blinked at us from a skull in the blackness as we approached it.

Eerily, our boat trudged along, every so often taking a pitched curve or an unexpected bump and scaring me from an overload of nothing but pitch black. Then suddenly, rounding a corner, our eyes beheld a life-size pirate ship, A swashbuckler with red beard on board cautioned us with raised sword while cannons blasted from the side portals. A feverish song rang through the air. "Yo ho, yo ho, a pirate's life for me." The tune was catchy and giddy and full of mischief. It made sense, especially since the following scene showed the pirates capturing village folks, tied up and scared to death. In contrast, the bandits broadly grinned. The pirate pals studied their loot, dresses and crates filled with all kinds of merchandise. They drank from barrels of rum, chased women mercilessly and gorged themselves on feasting foods. The red-bearded pirate showed up periodically throughout the storyline. Obviously, he was the ringleader. Finally, a big laugh came at the end when a dog sat with a key in its mouth where captured pirates, a reversal of fortune, begged for their freedom. Then just as we saw the proverbial light at the end of the tunnel, Grams and I pointed at a Jack Sparrow type pirate, coated from head to foot in gold and jewels. He was relishing in his newfound wealth. He was, indeed, the conqueror. I memorized that scene. I swore I saw gold and silver coins both, spilled all over the floor surrounding his booted feet. I had to get closer. I had to get pictures on my phone. But how?

By the time Grams and I disembarked, we located Mom on the edge of a garden wall nearby. Appearing mighty satisfied, her mouth was already wrapped around a half a sandwich. She wriggled the other half in the air as if to torment us.

"I want to ride that again," I told her and Grams. "Would you mind? It was awesome!" The two first tilted their heads in wonder then nodded. Knowing what they were contemplating, I added, "Don't worry. I'll eat as soon as I get back."

Both women happily agreed, now devouring their lunch and caring little about my desire. They nodded, placating me, then waved me off, but before I left them, Paulie tossed me an apple. My teeth gladly sunk into its juicy pink flesh.

This time onboard I had no company. My boat was completely empty and the boat behind me was nowhere in sight. The ride seemed so much longer than before. Maybe because I'd seen it already and nothing seemed new to notice. Like repeating an already watched movie, however, I did spot Jack Sparrow in two other scenes – at the well-dunking, he was hidden behind some other men, and then he was also hiding in a barrel, sneakily peeking at a treasure map held by a fellow pirate. Apparently, he was as mighty if not mightier than the red-bearded ringleader. Perhaps, he was much shrewder in his endeavors. In a way, I felt I somewhat resembled him. Finally, we reached Jack Sparrow in his personal glory, all by himself.

My boat and the scene's location were far apart, too distant for photography even when zoomed in. I was surrounded by water and had no idea how or where to get out to take pictures without getting wet. But I had to go for it.

I carefully slid my body overboard, making no splash at the left side of the boat then half-waded, half-swam over as fast as I could. I was soaked to the bone and pulled myself up onto the platform. Dodging quickly behind a fake wall, I watched as an oncoming boat passed by. Empty. Phew. Without a second to lose, I took out my cell phone and prayed it was protected enough to work. And work, it did. I shot at least two dozen photos of the booty around the room and even lifted a fake coin from the floorboard before I heard a booming voice yell, "Hey! What are you doing there? DO. NOT. MOVE!"

Uh oh. Caught.

I had no idea what that meant.

I hoped that I'd get only a tongue lashing and not get kicked out of the park.

Or my worst nightmare, I'd have to walk the plank.

8

MONEY MAKES THE WORLD GO 'ROUND

When I hopped off the bottom step into Vito's lair, I noticed a make-shift clothesline hanging across the cinderblock wall behind Peyton Manning. The cut-out was pushed aside and his eyes now staring at the photographs hanging near him. On closer look, I found different images of silver coins in each picture, not recognizable as U. S. currency. They most definitely were alien to our country. Fascinated by their odd shapes, my eyes combed over each page, scrutinizing their differences and similarities. I felt like Vito would grill me as soon as he made his appearance. He was a tough taskmaster, expecting everyone to be up to his high standards. I'd never measure up, but I knew he had a candidate in Beans. She didn't mind at all, being of same mind and interest.

The first four photos were stills and taken from an overhead view. Beans must've been awfully close because they were right on top of the floorboards. Their lengthy shadows ghosted the top layer of the bottom where distinct coinage spread out. One – two – three – four – five – six. Details were vague and undistinguishable. But the items overlapped one another in an odd fashion, as if being dumped there, not placed safely or separately. The next two photos answered my questions. Noticeable markings popped up, almost three dimensional. Cross-like etchings appeared on most. Unlike our silver dollars, half dollars, quarters, nickels, dimes and pennies, their edges were not rounded. Instead, they were jagged and, in many cases, flat and sharply cornered. The faces of them, if they were that side, were old, dark, tarnished and used. Probably, well circulated among people. Was it possible that these were, indeed, pirate doubloons? The clues from my observations certainly matched my reading material on the Internet.

After those came a series of stills taken from video footage. A few blurry images splashed their appearances on the copies, but they were more of the same, just peeking into a specific flash of detail, when even more zoomed in. My brain couldn't determine exactly what I was looking at, but it surely would add up to more collective information. Knowing Vito, he already had it figured out.

"B-Man," I heard his voice float down the stairway. "You down there?" his footsteps followed until he reached the cement floor. As he whizzed over, he summed up his findings. "You're checking out our girl's work, right?"

"Yeah," my response was obvious.

"Check out the ones down here on the other end," his clunky feet, too big for his body, sloshed along until he reached the end of the clothesline. He had on a roughed-up pair of Vans, black and white checkerboard in design. A big hole was at the top of his right foot. I assumed they belonged to one of his twin brothers and were a quick, convenient pull-on before he came downstairs to join me and continue his forensics work. "These were taken today from that pirate ride she went on. 'The Pirates of the Caribbean.' She did a fantastic job. Not sure how she got them, but she did great."

"Leave it to Beans to get the job done," I laughed and gave him a high five.

Vito crept up to the three at the end and ran his hand over the pages, "How the heck did she get onto this platform to get so close to these facsimiles? These replicas of the real thing are absolutely amazing! If they were put up against real doubloon in a museum, they'd pass as authentic to the naked eye."

The next few minutes, we settled at Vito's computer station where he already had the same images on the monitors. I reached into my side pocket and unfolded my notes, the ones I wrote at my dining room table. Little by little, I spilled every bit of knowledge I had about the silver coins and their history. Vito nodded along, studying my sober face and gestures as I emphatically and enthusiastically shared.

"Good work, Sherlock," his hand reached out and slapped the side of my arm. "Now, the real question is why are these coins beneath Beans' grandmother's floorboards? And who put them there?"

"Her grandmother," I volunteered. "It's obvious. She made an investment of some sort and is trying to hide them in a safe place."

"Naw, why not just lock them into her safe? I'm sure she has one. Every old lady and old man has one. Gees, even my parents have one bolted to their closet floor."

"Come to think of it," I said. "So does Pop." Then I considered carefully what I'd say next because the piece of information was confidential. Then I blurted, "Yeah, my old man's got his gun locked up in there. Not loaded though."

"Your old man has a gun?"

"Yeah, it's his sidearm from the Army. He only did one hitch . . . four years then he got out. Said he'd considered having a military career, but then he met my mom, and that was that."

Vito continued to size up what I was saying and merely bit his lower lip. I wasn't sure that he was even listening anymore, already devising a few theories to the stowed away money. Then I noticed him pulling his cell phone toward him, its vibration made the thing rattle against the metal countertop.

"Speaking of our girl," he held up his phone for me to see Beans name on the screen. "She's on FaceTime. Give me a thumbs up if you can hear her well enough. If not, I'll use this," and he pointed at a small metal tin that looked like it once held a row of sardines. Once he connected, he propped his phone up onto a wiry photo frame holder – another device used for a different purpose than what it was meant for. That was Vito, mother of invention. "Yo, girl. What's happening in the Mouse Kingdom?" he laughed. "You look a sight."

"Oh, nothing much. . . . other than being banished from the parks!" her frustration was mixed with anger as she grabbed a nearby brush and tamed her wild hair, fresh from a shower.

"What? No way?" I yelped.

"Oh yeah. I got into a little trouble for getting us the research needed."

Vito couldn't contain his laughter, "Unbelievable." His head shook back and forth like a baby's rattle. "What happened? Spill the beans, Beans? Sorry. Couldn't help myself."

Beans chucked the brush over her head then took a deep breath before unlocking the goods. Dying to tell us, her body repositioned itself and got down to the nitty gritty.

"Well, the day was moving along just fine. The three of us went on a bunch of cool rides in Fantasyland, ate a turkey leg for a snack then headed to the pirates' attraction. Every single ride was a blast, but that one was my favorite by far."

Typical Beans. Building up to the dramatic moment, I thought. Even though she appeared a bit disheveled, her face was radiant, glistening from a fresh scrubbing. We could only see the top of her chest, but she was wearing a pale lemon t-shirt with an outline of Mickey's ears and head. All the lines composed by tiny pink and white flowers along with green ivy vines. The colors showcased her shoulder length auburn hair. And those blue eyes of hers couldn't look any bluer.

She sounded good even though she was obviously ticked off at something or someone or maybe just the whole ordeal like I was with my summer shoplifting mishap. Now I wasn't alone with a bad guy record. Soon Beans, too, would be haunted by the nagging memory of an untimely misadventure.

Beans cleared her throat as she continued, "So, I got this brainiac idea to go back onto the ride a second time by myself. Paulie and Grams had no interest. They were too busy chowing down on lunch. They did toss me an apple when I went, though."

My neighbor had a way of prattling on with unnecessary details sometimes.

"Get on with it," I urged.

"Anyway, if I went on alone, I could make an attempt to get close up photos of the treasure chest scene. I hadn't planned on getting out of the boat. That was spontaneous. I knew I had to get onto the Jack Sparrow scene to take pictures of his booty. Well, not HIS body booty although that was cute – his loot, the byproduct of his notorious adventurous. Mounds and piles of coins were surrounded by jewels and jewelry plus other random trinkets pouring out of opened treasure chests." She let out a tremendous sneeze, sounding like Donald Duck. "Sorry. Some of the plants down here don't agree with me. Their fragrances are too strong." Then her eyes checked the perimeter before shaking her hair around and continuing her exploits, "When I realized that the boat ride didn't come close enough to the platform, I had to get over there, so I slipped out of my boat and waded, well, swam over to it. A poor imitation of the breaststroke. Anything to prevent splashing. It was only a few feet away. Just hard to do it fast without making noise, and then I had to hide from a boat that was coming before I took my dry cell phone out and snapped away." Her voice seemed nervous, repeating her actions. "I was so worried that a boat load of passengers would catch me on the platform."

"Let me guess," I said. "That's when you got caught."

"Boy, did I." Her tone shifted to exasperation and her mouth pursed with frustration. "I didn't realize what a big deal it was. All I intended to do was get back into an empty boat once one rounded the bend. I'd hide until then, of course, just so no other visitors would see me. And even though they didn't, how did I know that there were cameras all over the place?" She paused a minute, considering what she'd say next. "Obviously, Disney World security is all over the place, both outside and in. Who knew?"

Vito laughed again, "Honestly, Beans. A place as ginormous as Disney World . . . with all those valuables everywhere . . . ? That place is a gold mine for thieves. They have to protect their interests, especially from shoplifters and kooks. You know there are people who are so consumed by Disney everything that they'd do anything for a quirky souvenir to keep or, better yet, to sell on Ebay or at a flea market."

"Huh. Yeah, I never considered any of that. Oh well, lesson learned," she muttered.

Vito added, "And there are tons of security guards dressed like average looking visitors, too. You didn't know that?" But he didn't expect her to answer. In a way, it sounded like he was reprimanding her for not knowing. She was a smart cookie and it troubled him that she didn't realize the truth of her surroundings. "Lots of precautions there to protect their investments. They have to do that like any place of business."

"So, you were kicked out? I mean, right then and there?" I asked.

"Yup. I had to 'freeze' until two security guards and a cast member came onto the scene after shutting down the ride."

Vito jumped out of his seat, "They SHUT. DOWN. THE. RIDE? Holy smokes!"

"Um, yeah," Beans confessed with apologetic undertones. Her voice had a quiet lilt, "How did I know they'd do that? Let alone, kick us out?"

"Paulie must've been furious?" I said.

"That's an understatement," she declared. "She overreacted, in my opinion. Something about me dying under all the mechanisms that move the ride along under the water. Anyway, she immediately took away my phone as soon as she got me from the security building. Good thing I shot those photos to you while they escorted me out through the back corridors. It's so weird seeing the 'behind the scenes' frameworks and machinery. Not so magical," her sigh was intentional and dramatized her meaning. "And it seemed like it took forever until Mom and Grams got me. Besides, I was soaking wet and drying still."

Now Vito sat down again, "I can't even imagine."

"So, where are you now?" I asked, fidgeting with my notes paper, folding the corners into dog ears. "And whose phone is that?"

"We're all back in our hotel room at All Star Movies. We're allowed to stay tonight. But that ends out little mini-vacation." Her fingers covered the eye hole where the camera confronted her then she reappeared once more. "The phone belongs to Grams. She left it for me in case of an emergency."

"Where are they, your mother and grandmother?" Vito opened up his red composition notebook and drew a T-chart on the right-side page. At the top, he labeled, "Real. Fake."

"Paulie's in the back bedroom packing. We'll leave for Sarasota in the morning after breakfast. Grams said that she wants to at least get a little fun out of the trip since she organized it, regardless of my mother's mood. So, we'll have a nice dinner at a place she booked already then grab breakfast here at the hotel. They have an incredible spread." Then we could hear the unanticipated guilt in her voice, "I feel just awful. And, of course, Grams and I didn't tip our hands about the reason I took such a risk. Paulie has no idea about the hidden coins." There was deliberate silence for a few seconds, "Shhhh." She whispered. A minute later, "False alarm. Thought it was Paulie. So, where's my Grams? She went to the cashier room, or whatever it's called, to get reimbursed for the other two-day park passes. She prepaid for them online a month ago. The park officials said they didn't hold anything against her. And we could come back but wait at least a month or more."

"At least that's a good thing," Vito said. "You can go back one day."

"Maybe they were cutting you a break because you were visiting from out of state," I told her, trying to rationalize the park officials' decision.

"Yeah, but I spoiled everything. First time I get to come to Florida, and first time I get to go to Walt Disney World, and I blow it. I hope the two of them will forgive me," her sigh was much louder this time and sincere in its delivery. "Mom already told me that we're going to fly home a day early. That sucks." Her eyes welled up as if to cry. Then we heard a familiar voice in the background. "Oh, hi Grams. I gotta go, guys. I'll check in later."

I watched as my buddy leapt into action. My dog-eared paper now sat in his hand as he scribbled quickly under the two columns on his paper. Under the bolded word REAL, he listed: one inch in size; blunt edges, not symmetrical, diminished quality, tarnish, silver, age (?), eleven or twelve, thin, smooth faced, varied markings – Crusader's Cross, lion, castle. Then he switched over to the word FAKE: one and a half inch in size, circular / round edges, shiny like new minted coins, thick .25 inches, imitation cross, castle, lion, all the same. Vito took the eraser end of his pencil and scratched above his right ear then mumbled, "Interesting."

"What's interesting?"

"Disney went to great lengths to make their coins resemble the real deal the best they could. I heard that about their creative artists. Imagineers. But I'm guessing that the average guest's eyes would never be able to see all the tiny details on their coins in the ride's Jack Sparrow scene, so they cut corners and cheated a bit. But it all proves one thing," he said, "the ones in hiding are authentic. I'd stake my forensics equipment on it." As he said that, he propped his crossed ankles onto the rolling office chair next to him. "Now, I'm just wondering their value. We've got to research that still. You game?"

"I'm here, aren't I?"

Vito twirled his pencil between his fingers, passing it over and through then back again. Then he snapped a grin my way, "You know, Old Man Malloy used to be a dedicated numismatist."

Where'd I hear that word before. I couldn't remember.

"Don't look so puzzled, my man," Vito said. "Remember all the hubbub about that buried treasure in your backyard last fall? A numismatist helped us identify their worth." His hair was getting messy from all his finger combing and head scratching. "Anyway, he costs money. I'm broke after Fed Ex-ing that camera to Beans. Out eighty-five bucks, but it was well worth it. Look how far we got! Now, we need to check into Malloy's collection."

I was confused.

"But the old man died last year," my voice squeaked as I picked up a pencil from a blue glass jar on his counter. Then I attempted to glide my own pencil through my fingers. Major fail. The darned thing kept dropping onto the cement floor where I'd have to find it before trying again. "How we gonna find out about his collection? Did he have doubloons?"

Vito turned his hands into loose fists and rubbed both eyes with them, "I think he did. The only way we'll know thought is when you connect with Colin, his son."

"Me? Why me?"

Colin Malloy made me cringe, all full of himself and rich and hanging around Vito's Aunt Gracie all the time. He was most polite to me to a fault, and I always thought he was up to no good when I was around him. The man's wardrobe exceeded most in Mill Creek. Every piece of his outfits matched perfectly, from the top of his head to the tip of his toes. My dad called it "a snappy dresser," but my father would never be caught dead in anything fancy. His staple was jeans, t-shirts and Converse sneakers, the older style from his teenage years. Colin's successful real estate agency right on the outskirts of town had a reputation for fair sales and the most sales in the county. Certainly, his cut of each house sold or purchased made him a bundle over the years. And his dad's passing undoubtedly left him a hefty inheritance because Old Man Malloy was in the banking business, owning the local private bank that has since closed. The mansion in which the two lived, one never marrying and the other a long-time widower, was abundant with fine art paintings embellishing the rooms, exotic glassware, and vases from around the world plus so much more that my eyes had yet to see. I only had one occasion to visit Colin's father, and while he was more than hospitable to me, I could tell that he considered himself elite, better than me and my family. Unlike his only son, the old man didn't flaunt it or care about title and position in his final years. He spoke to me on the same level, recognizing that foregone days of clout were well behind him.

"Why NOT you? You've been to his house. You've worked in Aunt Gracie's store when he's been there. And besides, he likes you more than he likes me." My quarterback friend shrugged his shoulders at me, "You've got a certain charm about you, buddy."

The kind compliments fell on deaf ears.

"Well, if I do agree to go talk to him, just what am I supposed to ask?"

Tearing a page from his doodle notebook, the one where he sketched a silly image of a soggy Beans dripping next to a throned Jack Sparrow while she spoke to us on the phone moments ago, Vito scribbled a few notes for me. They included the following: What types of doubloons do you have in your coin collections? What's the one that's worth the most? How much do they go for on the market today? How do I contact current collectors? Do they hold their value?

"Oh, that's all?" I studied the paper once he placed it into my hand.

Vito's laugh was sinister, "Get going. No time like the present. He's probably by my aunt's store as we speak. You know he's over there on and off most of the day, any day of the week." His chair wheeled back to its regular spot in front of his main computer. "Aunt Gracie says he's actually a pretty decent guy. Personally, I don't see what she sees in him. He's not good looking at all."

Maybe Vito's aunt was all about the money, hoping one day he'd marry her and be well off. That way, the woman wouldn't have to keep working around the clock at her store. She'd be able to afford someone to run it for her, or better yet, sell the store all together. But then again, she didn't seem the type to be a gold-digger or unambitious or lazy.

"All right. All right," I said. "But you owe me, man."

He flicked his wrist at me as if to shoo me off and get me out of his hair.

Immediately, I located Colin Malloy at Aunt Gracie's as expected. I knew it once I'd seen his silver Porsche sidled up next to the curb by her shop. In a most cryptic way, I explained to him what Beans found and how interested we all were to find out more about the Spanish dollar, its history, its value, the works.

Not only did Mr. Malloy lend an intent ear, but he also invited me to ride over to his mansion to check out his father's investments. And I actually got to ride shotgun in his fast car.

Once we were inside his home, the man all stylish in his two-piece navy suit led me into his father's library. The room stood still in time. All the books on the shelves sat perfectly aligned, just as I'd remembered when I last spoke to Old Man Malloy. The eclectic collections of various nick-nacks situated themselves in matching encasements. Their wood, I speculated, was either mahogany or cherry. Nothing short of striking. A perfect choice to enhance the items inside the tall furniture pieces.

"Not too shabby," he smiled, his black moustache twitching above his thin upper lip. "My father had great taste in furniture and interior décor. That's mahogany wood," he mentioned, "If you wonder. Dad originally had cherry wood curios, but the sun darkened the wood grains too much in this room. So, he sold them. Got a pretty penny, too. Then he replaced them with these babies. They're a little more orange in color with the red, but they do the trick and went well with everything else in here." I nodded when he asked, "Don't you agree?"

As Colin spoke, his wingtips dragged over the oriental rug, vibrant in its burgundy and gold tones. Around its rectangular edges were creamy tassels, about two inches long. The room was about twelve by twelve so the rug, I assumed, was around eight by ten because it covered a huge space beneath my feet. The rectangular movement from edges to the middle was a typical pattern. Not that I knew much about decorating, but the rug complemented everything else in the room – from furniture pieces to artwork on the wall to the old man's favorite and somewhat beat up maroon recliner in the corner. It was the spot where he sat when we discussed the cold case at Mill Creek Bridge last summer. My heart sunk for a moment, recalling his kindness even though he seemed quirky in his mannerisms.

"Over here," Colin stood near three boxes hanging side by side against the dark wallpaper. They offset the standing curios across the room. "These shadow boxes have lots of goodies inside, some of my father's favorites."

His hands reached up and carefully lifted each off the wall. A darker shade of wallpaper remained beneath them, most likely from years of sunlight peering through the windows to illuminate the boxes while bleaching the remaining wallpaper around them. Then he walked over to the recliner and neatly stacked them, one on top of the other.

"Each case collectively displays around twenty-five- or thirty-coin slabs. If you observe, Dad chose matching mahogany to blend into the room. That man babied everything that he loved," Colin's voice sounded almost regretful.

"Coin slab?" I questioned out of ignorance.

The forty-something year old gentleman dug into his pants pocket and pulled out a small key ring. Tiny keys, much smaller than ones used for houses or cars, filled the two-inch circle of silver. He deftly flipped to a particular one on the ring then lifted up the top case. On its side was a built-in lock in which it fit perfectly. With one twist, Colin opened the display's door, encased in heavy glass. Then he lifted out a silver collar and handed it to me.

"This heavy plastic holder offers crystal-clear viewing for the collector or onlookers," he handed it to me. "It is scratch resistant, and you'll notice that you can view both front and back sides of any coin.

The black insert allows the actual coin to be noticed well." His long fingernail pointed above the inserted coin. "See this? The company even provides a blank card for descriptive information about the coin itself." Again, his finger emphasized the spot. "This is what's called a slab."

"Coin slab, you said?"

"Yes. The manufacturers for these special cases know well their numismatists."

There was that word again. Fancy word from a fancy man.

"If you look into the case now," he lifted it to me. "You'll see there are four shelves about an inch or so deep that sit safely behind the glass. Also, they have a subtle lipped edge that prevents the coin slabs from sliding off. Then the background is a simple black velvet glued against the wood itself."

Wow, I thought to myself. It was hard to imagine that so much detail was placed into a coin collection.

He noticed my facial expression, "You're probably thinking, boy, people sure do go to a lot of trouble and expense to show off their coins. Right? But think of it this way, Balthazar. If you're investing money into something that you hope will pay off with even more value and cash in the future, it's worth protecting."

"You're right," I said. "Of course. Makes sense. I don't think I'll ever be that rich to someday do any of this," I spun around the room, pointing and giggling, uncomfortably.

"Don't count yourself out, son," Colin put the case back onto the others. Then he lifted out two specific coin slabs. One held a gold coin. The other, silver. "You wanted to know what a doubloon looked like in real life, right? Well, here you go." And he handed the two to me for inspection. "Take your time. You want a drink or anything? I'm going to head to the kitchen."

I liked that the man trusted me. I mean, he was probably one of a few Mill Creek citizens who knew about my shoplifting CD boardwalk story, quite a personal fiasco. After all, he was dating Aunt Gracie who was the sister of Vito Rusamano's dad. As police chief, Pete Rusamano had a long reach with the law around all of New Jersey, Unfortunately, so was Rocky Wallace's. No doubt, Pete Rusamano shared the story about my dilemma to his sister or through his wife who conveyed it to his sister. Mill Creek was a rumor mill, rife with gossip like most other small towns. I loved where I lived, but I hated it for that.

The front side of the gold coin held wavy lines under two post-like elevations, vertically above them. Two lines moved through these, making a sort of tic-tac-toe pattern. Within the boxes up in the right side appeared an M, an A, and the number 8. The middle section lined top to bottom with an 8, a capital V and the letter I. Juxtaposing this at the left were a weird blemish of gold metal, a capital P, and the number 1. I had no idea what any of it meant so I flipped the slab over and immediately saw a cross. From the center, each arm resembled a capital T. Then inside the boxes, formed around them, were castles at top left and bottom right plus castles in the other diagonal corners. The cross, castles and lions jostled my memory with the recent research Vito and I did. The edges surrounding the coin itself were bumpy, not smooth at all with little divots taken out in spots. Again, like the description and images seen before this, the authenticity of the coin being a doubloon was dead on accurate.

Colin reentered the room and offered me a bottle of Coke. He was already sipping his, the twist off top gone and bottle's mouth meeting his.

"That's a beaut, isn't she?" he admired it in my hand.

"So, is this a real doubloon?" I had to ask in disbelief.

"Sure is," he said, taking another swig. "It's an escudo. From Peru. Circa 1718."

"Wow," my head ached thinking of how old that was, and I examined both sides once more. Two hundred and ninety-six years old. "But you called it an escudo. I thought it's called a doubloon. Did only pirates call it that?"

Colin grinned, "No, Balthazar. The doubloon was a slang term for two escudos, or double one escudo. The pirates seemed to adopt that name, but no one knows for sure the history of the name. Lots of written documents lead us to think that, yet not one of them hints at the date or age of the word. That's the only proof." He plucked the coin slab from me, "Did you notice the Herculean pillars and the ocean waves?" he pointed to the details on the coin's face. "And the numbers and letters, they signify when and where the coin was made in Peru. Cool, huh?" Suddenly, he guzzled down the last of the soda with three long gulps. Then he let out a loud burp. "Pardon me," he smiled, sheepishly. "The bubbles do it to me every time." I hadn't even opened mine yet, too intrigued with these treasures. "Getting back to the coin. Most doubloons have the Jerusalem Cross on them along with castles and lions."

"Yeah. I noticed," I said. "What's up with those? I mean, the cross, the lions and the castles?"

"Well, at the time, there was a close connection between religion and the government of Spain back in the 16th through 18th centuries. As for the lion and the castle, they represent the province of Leon and the province of Castille in Spain. They are still located in the northwestern region of the country. In history, they were the powerful administrative hot spots at the time and no doubt the places where these coin designs originated."

"But you said it's from Peru."

"Yes, but remember, Balthazar. The kingdom of Spain was powerful with its adventurous explorers traveling and conquering all sections of the world. Peru was conquered by the Spanish empire in the 16th century."

"Ah ha," was all I could utter. Then I placed the gold coin back into the box and studied the other silver one yet in my hand. "Was this one from Peru, too?"

"No," Colin stood next to me now, too close for comfort. I liked my personal space, and ever since Mr. Law and Order bothered me, I withdrew from people for safety's sake, not knowing what they might pull. "This one is definitely from Spain. Most likely it was recovered from a shipwreck or stolen from a cargo ship way back when. That front side is pretty worn, but you can still see the shield in the coat of arms. It was a common stamping. Represents the Hapsburg royal family. Now hold onto your hat," he told me. "That family name represented Queen Isabella and King Ferdinand."

"Wait! What?"

"You heard right," Colin suddenly emitted a boyish giggle. "You remember those names?"

"Of course! But no way? They were the royal couple who backed Christopher Columbus to explore. And he discovered America. Well, kind of," I said, recalling my history lessons. Isabella of Castille took a liking to the Italian adventurer and backed his journeys, longing to expand the Spanish empire.

Columbus was constantly turned down for funding long before Isabella and Ferdinand agreed to take the risk on him. Of course, power and greed were the royal couple's main motives, not a true interest in what America had to offer their kingdom and its people.

"Man," I said, now reaching for the Coke that Colin left on the end table nearby. "And the back is consistent with the gold coin. Another religious cross and more lions and castles. Wow, wow, wow."

The coin in this slab was well over five hundred years old. It was hard to fathom. And Columbus had to be around forty when he dared to take such a voyage. Maybe this coin went with him. It was a far stretch but anything was possible, and here it was, sitting in the palm of my hand.

Now for the hard question. Because I didn't want him to think I'd try to break in and steal these valuable coins.

"I'm not meaning to be nosey," I began. "This is still more research for what Beans found at her grandmother's house in Florida. What's the value of coins like these? They look like they're in good condition." I did know a little about the terms people used for investing. Mint condition means fresh out of the manufacturing process. Then it went down from there to poor quality. "I'm sure they're worth a pretty penny."

"Guess it all depends on who wants them and how much they're willing to pay for them. Also, how popular are they or how rare. If there

are more of the same, it diminishes their value as you can imagine."
Unexpectedly, Aunt Gracie's boyfriend gave me a side-eye, glancing at
my being and probably questioning my sincerity and integrity. "The
gold one is about twenty-six grams in weight and it's a good quality
standard. 24 Karats. A year ago today, it had a five-hundred-dollar
price tag on it. Today, with gold prices going up to sixty-three dollars
a gram, it's close to a thousand, seven hundred dollars. Again, possibly
more on who might want to add it to his or her own collection."

I didn't know what karats were. I immediately thought of rabbit
food, carrots instead. The man must've read my mind because he
explained how gold was measured by its flawlessness and purity. The
higher the number, the more the actual gold and less other metal con-
tent like nickel or copper or something else. Man, was I ever getting
schooled by Colin Malloy. More than I'd asked for, but I knew both
Vito and Beans would be pleased to hear all the juicy trivia.

"Gees, that's a ton of money for one coin!" I exclaimed.

"Indeedy," Colin smiled and removed the silver coin slab from my
hand while I glugged my soda, not realizing how thirsty I'd become.
"And this cutie, she's around fifty dollars. Silver is just under a dollar
a gram in today's market. My dad has about four of these, all in the
same condition between average and good. They're very popular by
not only collectors, but laymen like you or me. I'm guessing it's more
of a sentimental or emotional interest with folks."

"Gees," my voice showed its surprise. "I'm surprised it's not worth
more. But then again, I don't understand this market anyway. . . but
I'm learning."

He winked and added, "Plus there are the stories that come along
with a coin, especially the Christopher Columbus one. They add

value, too, even if there's no document of proof. People will believe what they want to believe, and that's good enough for them." His hand jostled the coin slab around, circulating the hard plastic in his palm. "You never know what this one could bring. . . especially to the less discernible buyer."

"I suppose," I said, confused by the word discernible.

My brain buzzed with thoughts of the eleven or dozen coins in Bean's grandmother's house.

"Listen, I can't thank you enough for all your time. Showing me all of this," I pointed to the cases on the recliner. "You need a hand putting these back up?"

Refusing my assistance, I watched as Mr. Malloy lifted them and gently repositioned on the wall, matching their appropriate shadowed locations on the wall.

We walked out together and, as he locked the heavy double oak doors, he gestured for me to climb into his car again. Riding in Colin's Porsche was sweet. The motor hummed like a well-oiled machine. I knew now what people mean when they said their engine purred like a quiet kitten. The smell of new leather lingered in the vehicle. I loved it and put it on my wish list for the future. A Porsche or a Corvette. I'd reach for the stars.

My personal chauffer parked alongside the variety store. As soon as we arrived, Aunt Gracie beckoned him inside, yelling, "Colin, honey. You have a phone call."

His face read disbelief as he checked the cell phone in his pocket.

"Dead as a doorknob. No wonder someone is calling me here," he shared with me, figuring he needed an explanation. "Okay, darling. I'll be there pronto. Just lock the door when you leave. Okay, buddy?"

Colin disappeared up the short stack of stairs and through the store opening. I heard the little doorbell sound off.

I walked around the sports car, examining the details with great joy. Vito wasn't expecting me at any particular time, so I figured I'd digest more of my ride's magnificence. Unbeknownst to me, a black SUV pulled up in front of my duplex across the street. It wasn't until I heard a flirtatious, squeaky voice call out my name.

"Hey, Booger," Drew called me, stepping off the front porch near Beans' entrance door. "Isn't Beans home yet?"

Officer Wallace rolled his window down on his police car. His eyes questioned my motives as I stood next to Mr. Malloy's automobile. I tried to fully focus on his daughter who was clearly flirting with me now.

"Not until tomorrow if I remember correctly," I piped up, remembering the fresh conversation I'd had earlier with Beans along with her changed return date.

"You busy now?"

"Right this minute?" I asked, still dodging her father's attention as he clamored out of his driver's side. He tugged off his cap and placed it under his arm before shutting the door. "Not this second, but I'm heading to Vito's." I watched as Mr. Law and Order checked the flow of traffic then jaywalked toward me. "He's expecting me," I emphasized.

Drew just shrugged her shoulders, "Well, you're missing out on some fun company. Thought we might grab a slice at Rivera's."

Just then, Officer Wallace blocked my view, deliberately standing between her position and mine. My back was literally pressed up again the Porsche. There was no escaping.

"Notching up your stealing skills, kid?" his voice hounded me. "CDs are nothing compared to Grand Theft Auto." Then he cleared his throat and spit a glob of saliva at my feet, barely missing my boots. "Trying to figure out how to do it in broad daylight, boy? That takes a lot of balls."

The man disgusted me. I merely got a ride to do my girl and best friend a favor, and here I was practically getting arrested. For nothing.

"Nothing like that, sir," I mumbled.

"Then what?" he antagonized me with his grilling efforts. "What are you doing hanging around Colin Malloy's expensive car?"

I had half a mind not to answer at all. What was I supposed to say? I was checking out the car just because I liked it. He'd never believe me. He wasn't willing to do so. He wasn't the generous type, never cutting anybody a break – probably not even his family.

Just then, I heard a hysterical voice calling my name, "Balthie. Balthie. Come. Come. Now. Now."

Then I heard a tiny voice repeat the same words, "Come, Balthie. Come now. Come now!" Haddie excitedly yelped as she followed my grandmother to the sidewalk from out our front door. "Satan! Satan!"

I hardly recognized my grandmother. Babcia's hair was a lavender white and short and very curly.

"You okay, Babcia?" I rushed past the police officer, practically knocking him over. "What's wrong? And what did you do to your hair?"

Babcia was breathing heavy as she tugged my arm, "Satan. Dog run off. Hole in fence. Backyard. He go. He run. Babcia no chase. Dog too fast. Babcia too old," her explanation was solid, but she was overexcited, so I helped her onto the porch step to sit with Haddie.

"I'll get him, Babcia. Don't you worry," I promised her and kissed my sister's forehead because I could see that she was worried, too. "He's probably down by the bridge, sniffing out other dogs."

"I'll come with you," Drew volunteered to the demise of her father who frowned strongly in our direction. "I'm not doing anything anyway. Two sets of eyes and feet are better than one."

Her obvious motive hit me over the head like a sledgehammer. I knew she liked me. Beans told me about her crush around Thanksgiving time, but I didn't think of Drew in the same way. I didn't want her to tag along, but for the sake of avoiding her old man, I welcomed her assistance.

9

TINKLE, TINKLE, LITTLE COIN

Darkness was gradually rolling in as our car covered the final miles to Sarasota on Route 75 South. Barely a word left anyone's mouth after we exited the Walt Disney World compound. Grams convinced Mom to stick around after brunch. Her explanation for the extension was so her only granddaughter could experience a heated pool in wintertime. My Grams could pour it on thick when she had to, and I loved her clever maneuvering. Very tricky. It reminded me that we shared our mutual DNA. She said she'd ask for a late checkout time then all of us could hang at the All-Star Movies' pool with the *Fantasia* Mickey and dancing mops presiding. My grandmother created one excuse after another, providing more time for me to enjoy what little time we had on our mini-getaway. Paulie, on the other hand, went on strike and remained most of the time in our hotel room, graciously delayed to a lackadaisical 2PM. All the while, my grandmother and I munched on goodies from the World Premiere Food Court, the resort's handy restaurant. First, we downed pickles-in-a-pouch then chicken strips with spicy barbecue sauce and, finally, hummus with celery sticks and carrots. Grams also hit up the Silver Screen Patio Bar behind our lounge chairs for a frozen margarita or two. Good thing Mom didn't know. She wouldn't approve, knowing we were driving home before dinner. For me, Grams delivered Dole Whip smoothies. Delightful pineapple, custardy milkshakes, in my opinion. But the first one did give me a brain freeze.

I knew the silence in the car was attributed to my bad behavior, but surely the day at the pool made Grams and me exhausted, too tired to make a peep. The intense sun in Florida drained our energy, adding to being already emotionally drained. Quite frankly, I was tired of apologizing so many times. Grams readily forgave me. Paulie, not so much. She repeatedly told me, "I'm so disappointed in you, Quinn. So disappointed." Then she announced that because of my poor behavior, she was cutting our trip at Grams short. That meant we would leave tomorrow instead of Friday. That was a major bummer. We only arrived Monday and had a day at the beach. Then only Tuesday at Walt Disney World instead of the original two nights and three days there. I didn't need to be in the land of the celebrity mouse and his friends. I only wanted to experience fun adventures in Grams' neighborhood and at the beach. Any time spent with Grandma Firenzi was magical to me. She was my world. That was probably why she decided to manipulate the pool time at our hotel before heading out.

My eyes glared at the back of my mother's head who decided to drive, accusing my grandmother of being tipsy. Grams denied the accusation, and I didn't blame her. I'd seen her guzzling bottles of water with me in between her only two cocktails, one of which was halfway consumed. Mom's signature low ponytail in black scrunchie managed to communicate "back to the old grind" mentality. As far as vacation goes, she had already checked out. In fact, her fingers busied herself in the hotel room on her personal taxi app, tying up her returning days with book-ended airport trips. The notion that she wanted to be more at work than with Grams and me on fun outings weighed heavily on my brow. Mom needed this trip as much as I did, or for that matter, Grams did. We all needed to "feel the love" of family for a while, to regroup and consider what was most important in life.

Finally, Paulie flipped on the blinker and turned onto Grams' Street. Her house quickly came into view, and I was relieved to be there. In the spacious house, I wouldn't feel trapped in a cloud of my own guilt like I experienced in my grandmother's backseat.

When we pulled into the driveway, Mario was quick to greet us.

"My girls are back early," he declared, sporting an open button-down flamingo shirt. His muscular biceps glistened at the edges of his short sleeves. "I didn't expect you until tomorrow night. What gives? Everybody okay?"

Ever the gentleman, Mario clomped to the back of Grams' Audi, waited for the gate to lift up, then grabbed all our bags. He placed them onto the freshly power-washed driveway and then picked up the Igloo cooler. Once he had everything in order, his clogged feet led us to the front door where he insisted on unlocking it and putting everything inside. We followed as if he was a personal bellhop at a fancy hotel.

"You want these in your room, babe?" Mario juggled all four things in his arms while he consulted Grams.

Babe, I thought to myself. Grams keeps saying Mario is a good friend, but I was beginning to see it differently. And I thought it was wonderful. He knew where her bedroom was and that spoke volumes to me. They genuinely loved each other, cared about one another, looked out for each other. That was grand. But my face fell upon my mother's, and she was wearing a frown. Obviously, she didn't approve of their intimacy. And I didn't understand why.

Grams giggled like a little girl, "It's fine, honey. You can leave them by the hallway. We'll manage the rest." The man sauntered over and lined up the satchels. "And thanks for doing the driveway. Turned out beautiful. Spotless." As he waltzed past her, Grams stopped him and he bent down, all six feet two of him so she could kiss his cheek. Mario practically blushed before he headed toward the front door. "And thanks for keeping an eye on the plants. They don't look thirsty or dead like last time," she tormented him, apparently recalling a time past when Mario ignored his promised caretaking duties. Maybe it was when she was up staying by us last November and December. "Not a very nice Christmas gift as I remember."

My calculations were correct.

"All right. All right," Mario's face scrunched up with delight. "I deserved that. So, for my penance, does my Queen need anything else addressed before I go?"

The older woman's head shook no and played along.

"Be gone," she tossed her hand in his direction. "Get thee home."

As Mario's feet exited the doorway, he added in haste, "That darn tile company van was lurking around again last night. Not sure what that's all about. But once I came over to put your porch light on, it took off. Maybe," his brown eyes twinkled, "just maybe, one of those dudes is sweet on you. But he better watch himself. I'll knock his block off."

Both of them let out an uproarious laugh before she lightheartedly slammed the door behind him.

"That man is so much fun," Grams said, grabbing her bag and heading down the corridor.

My mother said not a word. With great intent, her hands gently lifted and placed the cooler into the kitchen sink where she quickly rinsed it out. Then she reached beneath and removed the drying rack from the cabinet and turned the unit upside down on it to air dry on the counter. When she was done, her eyes confronted mine for a good minute or two. Afterwards, she whirled off, whisked her bag from off the floor then retreated to her room.

Man, oh man. She was boiling mad. The silent treatment was a major indicator. These moments rarely happened between us, but I knew I was in store for a couple more days of it before Paulie might soften up and forgive me.

The quirky clock centered on the wall above the sink read 5:55.

Artistic touches made my grandmother's home fresh, cozy, and interesting. The clock's face was set in the middle of a silver mixing bowl, and the kitchen mixer was in the "on" position with its blending tools inside, working. Scarlet red, its body marked its noteworthy attention to anyone inspecting the details of the room. Beneath the bowl, however, was an unexpected surprise - - a white icing topped cupcake sitting within a red and white striped paper holder. Its cherry on top attached itself to a swinging pendulum. The vision was fun loving and cute, adding a pop of color to the gray, creams, blacks, and silvers of the kitchen décor. As the minutes clicked away, the pendulum moved right then left, right then left, marking time.

Twilight settled around me, so I sat in Grams' special chair, the one by the investigative spot on the floor, and turned on the lamp. The abundant seashells within its glass body lit up with sparkles and lights. On closer inspection, I traced a wire line that twirled from top to base among the baby conch shells, whelks and sand dollars. They were easy to recognize after all the Florida postcards Grams sent to me. I couldn't wait until tomorrow when we would practice our Sanibel

Stoop. My grandmother told me all about it and even demonstrated on FaceTime, sticking her little round rump in front of her phone to bend over, pretending to pick up shells. Then she'd wriggle it just to make me laugh. Of course, we wouldn't drive south to Sanibel Island. We could readily practice the move and find shells nearby on Siesta Key beach, a "stone's throw away from here," according to Grams.

The house was quiet. Paulie and Grams hunkered down in their rooms respectively, no doubt watching television. I pulled my laptop from my backpack that I'd stuck on the floor beside me and checked my emails. My phone battery was on ultra-low and now charging on the kitchen island. But I was disappointed. No updates or communication from either Booger or Vito. I thought maybe I should call one of them, but then again, my phone would only die in the midst of a conversation. So instead, I decided to reexamine the photos and videos that I'd sent to Vito from his super-duper camera.

In the lower left-hand corner, I scrolled to the word "photos" and clicked on it. Immediately, I emersed myself in the old-world order, the one enveloping mystery and power. The collection of coins, now undeniably doubloons, were right under me, waiting for me to make our acquaintance. But I couldn't remember Booger's tips about how to loosen the tile boards. They were within his texts that I saved on my phone, but again, the phone was recharging. I checked the kitchen clock again. 6:15PM. Only twenty minutes had passed. I figured I would close my eyes and catch a few winks before my phone would be ready then I could return to my investigation. Pick up where I left off. And we'd all be ready for dinner. Maybe then, the deep freeze would've have thawed between my mother and me.

*   *   *   *   *

Through the foggy slits of my eyelids, I tried to refocus in the darkness. There was a dull clinking and rattling then a clicking that had awakened me. I assumed that when my eyes fully opened, Mom or Grams would be standing in the kitchen, prepping our dinner meal, and possibly grabbing a drink. But no one was there. The sounds ceased for a little while before starting up again. When the noises continued, intermittently, I stared at the front door. I worried that someone might be trying to break in, but I swore my grandmother set her alarm before she went to her room a couple hours earlier. Even if only at a glance, I knew I'd seen her fidgeting with the white rectangular box between the front door and the hallway entrance. So, if a random stranger was at the front door, the alarm would be going off. Instead, there was silence.

Readjusting my body which was achy all over from napping awkwardly in the chair, I continued listening acutely. The noises didn't remind me of anything familiar, but I kept hearing it at five-to-ten-minute intervals. My phone patiently sat on the island counter still, not within reach, and I feared moving just in case there was another body lurking.

Suddenly, I heard a long swoooooosh. And abruptly, my chair pushed forward as if by magic. What in heavens was happening to me?

"Aqui. Si. Si. Abajo," a low-pitched male voice whispered, not far from my ear.

Whoever was here was standing right behind me now and had no idea that I was stuffed into Grams' favorite recliner. I practically held my breath while I continued to listen, my heart pounding so hard that I feared that the mystery visitors could hear it and give me away. A tiny, noticeable light saturated a spot on the floor not far from the chair's bottom. The circle of white contained itself within an area of four inches in diameter. Whoever was at the other end of the light obviously knew exactly what he was looking for. I immediately realized he was here for the hidden coins. And maybe, just maybe, the silver sliver was deliberately rigged to remind that person of that location.

A different voice now asked a question, "Dame eso. Pronto." Another man, according to my keen hearing, had no patience. Instead, he sounded brash and rude and intimidating. "Ahora, Alvaro. No temenos tiempo."

An object rattled onto the floor. It sounded metallic and tinny.

"Tonto. Callado," the demanding voice said. "Aureate!"

A distinct scraping sound followed while the impatient voice urged the other to "hurry, hurry" in English. French was my second language from studying in middle school. But I did recognize the Spanish language when it was spoken. I just did not know the vocabulary at all. I could only imagine that they were calling each other names or aggravating each other, being in such a rush not to get caught in the house that did not belong to them.

I knew I had to get to my phone as fast as possible, but I could not run the risk of having them catch me. I had no idea what kind of criminals they were. For all I knew, they had concealed firearms on them or switchblades, sharp ones that could slash a little girl's throat in a heartbeat. I wasn't about to find out.

My body had to get out of the chair without them detecting me. That was going to be a challenge because the chair was a rocking recliner. Automatically, its frame would release itself and make a mechanical noise with its gears underneath when I'd get up. So, I devised a clever plan. I would turn myself around in the chair, hang my feet off the front seat and push all my weight forward as if to trick the chair into thinking I was still sitting there. Then ever so gradually, I'd release and lower my body to the floor in front of me without making a sound.

Summoning my courage, I counted to twenty-five then went for it. Once my feet touched the floor, I gently pulled my hands across the seat until they reached the front edge of the chair cushion. Still applying pressure up until the last minute, I finally dared to let go, lowering my snakelike body onto the floor and curled up into a fetal position. Not a sound occurred, and no reaction from the thieves behind me. The chair had been fully cooperative, and I was grateful.

I checked the distance between my location and the kitchen island. Fortunately, my cell phone sat at the end closest to the corridor. If I could only get over there, I could chase down the hallway into my bedroom and call the cops.

The scraping sound continued, more vigorously than before and nonstop. I heard the sliding glass door swoosh open again, signaling me that one person left. This was my perfect opportunity to sneak over since the other guy was steadily working on the floor. My body did an army crawl in a huge loop around the living room until I reached the front door then the hallway opening. At that point, I saw a shadowy body, about five feet small and chunky like a stubby pineapple, slide through the lanai slider. I knew it couldn't see me because I was smushed up against the wall, stretched out on the floor like an eel along the wood trim. As he crouched down to join his friend, I methodically used my toes to lurch my body forward. The process was slow but got me to the side of the island in two minutes flat. When I reached up to grab my phone, I accidentally bumped into a stool. Luckily, it did not fall and did not make a sound.

Continuing my stealthy maneuvers, I slid backwards on my backside, down the hallway until I reached my room. There, I quickly punched in 911.

"911. What is your emergency?" said a bright and cheerful lady on the other end.

"We have a break in. Two men, I think that's all, came in through the back sliding glass door." I tried to remain calm and not panic or prattle on nonsensically like Booger said I did. "They've been here about ten minutes."

"Where are you located, miss?"

"I'm in my grandmother's house. The guest bedroom in the back." Then I thought for a minute, "Well, technically not in the back. If you face the house," I explained in a hushed voice, "My grandmother is in the front at the right. My room is across the hall in the back of the house. My mom is in the one right next to me." I rambled a bit, "Also in the back."

"That's good, but that's not what I meant. You stay put where you are. What's the address of the house?"

"Hmmmm. Good question. I'm not sure. Hold on."

I didn't want to wake up Grams, but I had no choice. Her door was ajar, so I tiptoed in and went right next to her face. I gently jostled her shoulder.

"Sorry to bother you, Grams. But what is your street address?"

Without asking anything more, Grams merely opened her eyes a little and said, "1211 Pindo Palm Lane." Then she turned over and repositioned herself to fall back asleep.

I remained at the foot of the bed and told the lady waiting on the phone.

"Okay. Sounds like someone else is there with you. You are not alone, am I right?"

"Correct. I'm at my grandmother's like I said. She is here and so is my mom."

"All right," the woman said, softly and calmly. "And what is your name, young lady?"

"Quinn," I told her, thinking I better use my real name instead of my nickname.

"Well, Quinn," she said. "An officer should be there in about ten minutes. Stay on the phone with me until then, can you do that?"

I pulled my cellphone away from my ear a moment to check the battery cells. About eighty percent charged. I was good to go.

"Sure," I said.

In the meantime, Grams reawakened and sat right up on her bed.

"Good, Lord, honey. What's going on?"

"There are two men out in the living room. One called the other Alvaro. I don't know who the other one is," I explained to her, moving toward her door to close and lock it.

Bolting from her bed, Grams rushed to her chest of drawers and first grabbed her cell phone then dug around in her top drawer. Out came a small brown box, no bigger than five inches around. She propped open the lid and lifted from a black bag a small pistol. The revolver had a silver barrel and nose with a white glimmery pearl grip. Grams checked inside it before using her cell phone. She laid the gun on her bed.

"Don't touch that, sweetie," she warned me. "I'm calling Mario."

Once she had Mario on the phone, she was satisfied with sitting with me at the end of the bed, the gun and phone resting in her lap.

"Shouldn't we call or text Paulie?" I asked her.

"Your mom always sleeps with her door locked so she'll be just fine," she assured me. "Anyway, if we tried to call her right now, the noise might alert those criminals out there."

I hadn't thought of that.

"You stay here, Grams," I said. "I'm going to sneak down the hall and see if they're still here." I'd forgotten that the lady on the emergency dispatch was listening in, and I heard in the distance, "Don't do that, miss. Stay where you are."

But I needed to know.

Carefully, I unclicked Grams' doorknob lock and again slid my body, all scrunched up into a tinier version of myself, along the inside wall, taking care not to make a peep.

"Donde estan, Alvaro? Apurate! Apurate!"

That impatient man continued to badger his friend. Suddenly, I noticed a huge stream of bright light coming through the front bay window. The burst of white light covered the room and explored the area from ceiling to floor and wall to wall.

"Someone is here," I heard the frustrated voice proclaim. "Vamanos."

His partner screamed, "Pero los huesos. The bones, the bones."

Clank went the scraping tool, and the sliding glass door slammed wide open. Out rushed the two burglars. Then I suddenly heard, "You're going nowhere, hombre!" A familiar voice. Mario. With the cell phone still in my hand, I could hear the 911 lady ask, "Are you all right? What's happening? Are the police there now?"

"No, ma'am," I informed her. "It's my grandmother's neighbor."

I approached the lanai and peeked outside. The stumpy man that I had spotted earlier in the shadow was struggling under Mario's muscular frame. Mario was straddling him and pinning down his arms onto the landscaping stones. As Alvaro, I supposed, tried his hardest to escape, I caught the flashing red lights of the police pulling up in front of the house. They pounded on the door, so I ran over and unlocked the deadbolt and door lock. They ran in, and I pointed outside through the lanai where the policemen took off. The scene was a flash of activity and racket, enough to wake up my mother.

"For the love of Pete," she yawned. "What is going on here?" She tugged down her Springsteen nightshirt and stood barefoot in disbelief. "What did you do now?"

Annoyed with her false accusation, I responded, "Not much, just saved the day." I couldn't help that my voice was a bit snarky. "I'm a hero," and like the smarty-pants that I could sometimes be, I dusted off my shoulders and grinned at her.

Grams clamored out of her own bedroom, gun pointed in her hand and bypassed my mom and me, yelling, "Mario? Honey? Are you all right, dear?" And she rushed her body through the back door. Her short nighty showed off her knobby knees and chicken legs. But the rest of her was curvaceous and slamming, like the body of a thirty-year-old. She kept in great shape overall for a seventy-three-year-old lady. "Mario? Talk to me."

Mario groaned as he got up and gave way to the Spanish speaking dude.

"I'm fine, darlin'," he told her, removing the little pistol from her hand and tucking it into the stretchy waistband of his baggy sweat-shorts. "Got one of the bad guys. Hey, this thing isn't loaded, is it?"

"Naw," Grams said. "I have bullets, but they're locked up in the safe."

"Good to know," he grinned at her. Then he stared at me and Paulie. "You two okay?"

"Fine," Mom said, spying at me.

"Yeah, I'm good," I said. "That sure was exciting, wasn't it?"

The two policemen returned to the front door and began their inquiry. As they spoke to the adults, I slinked over to the floor tiles, now opened to reveal eleven silver coins. Keeping an eye on the five of them on the front porch, I scooped them up and deposited them inside the black planter in the corner behind the recliner. Its plant was a golden palm. I only knew that because Grams had inadvertently left its tag on it near the inside base.

The coins tinkled when I dropped them in. I'd get back to them later. If not tonight, tomorrow morning.

After all, finders' keepers. I found them first.

Well, me and Grams.

10

TIME TO CLEAN UP

The four of us hovered over the doubloons that now formed a precise line on my coffee table before us. Vito only muttered in disbelief about how old they possibly could be. He would run a carbon test or whatever he called it on them later on. Beans sat between me and Haddie. My friend kept saying, "Where did they come from? Where? Where?" Then my seven-year-old sister kept pretending to be a pirate repeated in a nonstop loop, "Arrrrr, maties. Me pirate's booty." All the while, she matched the coins by their patterns with the shields on the front and then flipped them over, only to match the Crusader's Crosses, linking their arms together. And me, I stared at the shiny objects and compared them in my memory to the two that I saw at Colin Malloy's mansion. Here they were, duplicates of Old Man Malloy's but tangible and free, the eleven trappings of Beans' grandmother's living room floor. They were possibly four or five hundred years old if they truly were real, authentic Spanish doubloons. And like my next-door-neighbor, I couldn't help wondering where they had come from and why the burglars decided to stash them at her grandmother's home.

Vito popped open his iPad from its jacket and began fooling around.

"Whatcha lookin' for?" Beans asked, inquisitively peering beyond me and squinting at his screen. "Grams didn't think it would be a big deal for me to keep them. But Mom doesn't know. She'd have a hissy fit if she found out. And she's already not talking to me still," she sighed.

"They've got to belong to some place or someone," Vito said, convinced that the thieves did not randomly discover them then tucked into the tile floorboards. "The news down in the Sarasota area must have covered it on television or a subscription newspaper. I'm thinking they were a part of a museum display, one of those touring events like The Titanic that most likely is at a downtown historical building or art gallery. Something like that. These dudes thought they were valuable and decided to take them. A spontaneous act, no doubt. But I don't think they thought any farther than that," Vito plugged in a few phrases and terms to search for the details. "They probably needed valuables to cash in on. Who knows? But we'll soon find out."

Haddie clamored off the couch, her tiny Dora the Explorer sneakers touched down safely before scurrying off toward her toy chest against the dining room wall. Suddenly, one of her shoes caught the corner of the area rug. As a result, her body crashed to the floor and her sneakers lit up on their soles.

I rushed over to help her, 'You okay, kiddo?"

"Arrrrrr," was all she said at me then made a sharp turn toward her chest and opened its lid. "Need sword. Sword protects pirate booty. Arrrrr." Her hands dipped inside and rummaged around the costumes, toys, stuffed animals until she pulled out a gray plastic sword, the swashbuckling type with a large black handle. The blade was safe but long and broad. "Arrrrr." But Haddie didn't seem happy. Her mind was racing with an idea, but she couldn't figure out what to say.

My helpful hints usually worked so I began, "Do you need a pirate's outfit?" I scrambled over to the toys and searched. I did not remember her having one, but that did not prevent me from lifting the assorted items and examining the treasures. "Is it a hat, Haddie? Do you have a pirate's hat in here?" Her head stared at the chest, and she didn't budge. "Another sword? Do you have a different sword? Or maybe a bandana for your head?"

Without saying a word, my little sister lifted her right hand and placed it over her right eye. Her face studied mine, locking eyes of serious intent.

"Oh, an eye patch? Is that what you want? An eye patch?"

Haddie shook her head and dug through her toy chest again. Together we finally found a black felt eye patch on a thin elastic cord. I had forgotten that it was in there, probably because Haddie dressed up more often as a Disney Princess or Chef than a pirate. But with today's coins from Beans, Haddie was motivated to pretend to be a pirate. Once she had her mind made up, there was no changing it. But that was okay. It made Haddie happy for a couple hours or more, and we all loved seeing her use her imagination.

Satisfied with how I adjusted her eye covering, Haddie took off for the kitchen to join my grandmother. I could hear Babcia singing one of her favorite songs in Polish. From the time she joined our family four years ago, she tried to teach it to me, but my tongue couldn't wrap itself around the words in her Polish language. But I did know that the song was about her home country of Poland, its beautiful green countryside and old castles. The words as they poured from her mouth made her face light up with immense joy. At times, I felt bad for my grandmother, knowing that she missed her homeland and had no idea when she'd ever go back to visit. Haddie sang along, skillfully imitating our Babcia's accent. The little girl practically knew every single word. As Babcia prepared pierogies for our dinner and for the freezer inventory, Haddie sang along and swished her mock blade through the air on the downbeat.

"Ah ha," Vito said with Beans practically jumping into his lap to read what he was reading. "I told you so." His boney index finger tapped vigorously at the monitor. "Says here that the doubloons were taken from a local exhibit."

I flopped back onto the couch alongside Beans and listened as she read aloud.

At approximately 2AM Monday night, February 18, police discovered a breached door at the back of Downtown Art. The gallery exhibit for the month highlighted two-hundred artifacts, documents and paintings of pirates owned by local artisans and collectors. Eleven coins among facsimiles were stolen from a glass encasement near the back of the boutique. Owners believe that the culprits knew exactly what they were looking for. "Two ruby pendants and a gold crucifix from the 19th century were also taken and have yet to be found," stated Aubrey Hughes, co-owner of Downtown Art that underwent building renovations at the end of last year and just reopened. "We are offering a reward in conjunction with the owners who also have three valuable paintings of Jean Lafitte on exhibit." Police found no fingerprints at the scene and continue to gather information from the general public. Anyone who might have information should contact the Sarasota Sheriff's Office as soon as possible."

Vito shook his head harshly, "I hope they're checking all the surrounding security cameras on local business buildings. There's still a window of a chance to match up the guys who were at your grandmother's with whomever took the gallery's stuff."

Pirate Haddie rushed into our space, yelling "Housekeeping. Housekeeping. Clean up. Clean up." Her sword swept down to move the coins off the table, and as they landed on the rug below, she ran off as quickly as she'd sped into the family room.

"What on earth?" Beans shook her head. "Your sister is . . . . ," grasping for the right word to say, "Interesting. That's for sure."

Vito stared off at Haddie's exit then paused a moment before turning to Beans and asking, "Hey, question. Didn't your grandmother have a security system at her house? She's an old lady who lives alone. Even Aunt Gracie has one installed now after her last problem, and she's thirty years younger than your Grams."

I watched as Beans squirmed next to him.

"Yeah, you would think so," Beans began. "I thought she did because when we came home from Walt Disney World and came into the house with Mario, she went over to the wall unit to see it. Then I found out after the break-in that the box on the wall regulates the air conditioner. It's one of two thermostats. Grams had set back the temperature inside to 78 degrees. That way the air conditioner wouldn't kick on as much when we were away. But she also set the heat on 64, just in case the temperatures dropped at night. Good thing she did, too, because it got chilly - - in the 50s while we were at All Star Movies."

Vito kept pressing, "But you sent us a text and photo of you standing in front of your Grams' house when you arrived. Right at the end of the walks from her front door to the street is a red post in the ground that states 'Smart House Security System. Warning. 24 Hour Surveillance.' Did I see wrong?"

I could tell that Beans was impressed by his keen observation. Somehow, I had missed it.

"Yes, that's right," she bubbled over. "And I thought that meant she did have one. Come to find out, a woman friend who plays poker with her has a husband who puts in security systems for Smart House. He gave her a sign to put into her lawn until Grams can afford to put a system in. Of course, she'll use his service."

Clever woman, I figured. But unfortunately, the boys who broke in were wise to her. They had to be the guys that laid the floor tiles a few weeks ago. And they were opening up the flooring just like Andy Clark told me in his store. The robbers were using a tool to scrape the grout out then loosen the tiles to lift and shift them. Clark's Hardware Store seemed to always have the right answers for the community. The store was small but mighty, better than Home Depot and Lowe's.

Beans got up for a minute to stretch her back and neck.

"Mom and I found out from Mario, too, that Grams is kind of lazy about checking the locks on her doors at night. Apparently, she nods off in the living room then just heads into bed. Doesn't turn the lights off or anything. Mario has often stopped in, unannounced, to do it for her. He even locks the back sliding doors. Fortunately, he has a key to the front door so he's able to check in on her or the place."

"She's got to be more careful," I offered. "None of us wants anything to ever happen to her. Your Grams is far too nice a woman to get hurt by a stranger."

Beans shook her head after brushing her reddish bangs off to the side of her temple, "She's far too trusting. I've told her that way too often. Me, I don't trust anybody or anything until I have enough evidence collected to do so. Maybe that's going overboard, but the world today is a far more dangerous place than when my mom or Grams grew up."

We all nodded in agreement.

The three of us were quite the sight, all dressed in black as though we could've been cat burglars, too. Black jeans or sweats with black hoodies. Our only distinguishing difference covered our feet. Beans with her imitation brown Uggs, Vito with his checkerboard Vans and me in my black moccasins with the turquoise beaded Phoenix.

"Say, why don't we call her?" Vito suggested. "We can fill her in on that article."

Beans leapt up, darted off through the front door and into hers with a slam. We could hear her feet stamp up her staircase and overhead. In just as short a time as it took her to go home and grab her laptop, she was back.

Her home screen contained the icon for Skype, so she clicked on it. We huddled around her, waiting for her grandmother to connect. Lo, and behold, Grandma Firenzi's face lit up the screen.

"Hiya, Grams," Beans smiled in seeing the older woman. "You're looking great, and I miss you already . . . so, so much." She lifted her hands from the keyboard and placed them to her lips then threw kisses the woman's way. "Do you miss me?"

"Of course, sweetie," Grams said, applying Chapstick to her lips then smacking them. "I missed you the second you got out of my car at the airport departure gate." Her face came incredibly close to her cellphone, almost kissing the screen. When she backed up, the woman wrinkled her nose at us, "Miss you a ton."

"Awwww, thanks, Grams."

Mrs. Firenzi's eyes jumped right and left, "I see you have company, Quinn. Who are those handsome gentlemen? I think I know but why don't you tell me anyway."

She didn't have to because Vito spoke up.

"We only met once, ma'am," Vito said, "When the fire gobbled up the roof of Meyer's Bakery." Then he clumsily wrapped his arm around my shoulder, "And you know my buddy, B-Man. I mean, Balthazar. Beans' neighbor."

The woman pursed her lips like a fish and made a kissing sound.

"You boys look more handsome than I remember," she was flirting with us now, and I found that weird but funny. "No wonder my grand-daughter is in love with you two. Not only are you good-looking, but you're also both smart as whips. Sadly, you're much too young for me."

"Hey there," Mario joined her on the screen, peering over her left shoulder. "Remember me? I'm the good looking one on the screen over here."

Grams playfully slapped his face, "Get out of here, you!"

The woman was sitting on a stool at her kitchen island, according to Beans, so Mario must have been near her or in her living room within reach. I could tell my soon-to-be girlfriend was surprised by that but pleased at the same time.

"What's all this racket?"

My dad came out from his room around the corner from our family room.

"Pop? What are you doing home? I had no idea you were even in there," I told him while Vito and Beans made small talk with her grandmother. "You look awful," I got up and met him as he headed toward the kitchen.

Stan Bugerowski always had firm footing and a robust complexion but right now, my father looked frail and piqued, wobbly on his feet and dizzying. I took him by the elbow and led him back to his bedroom.

"I'm parched," he complained to me. "I was going to get some Gatorade."

"I'll take care of that, Dad," I assured him. "You climb back into bed."

"Came home from work early," he managed to say with little energy. "Must be a 24-hour bug. It's going around at the store. Lucky me."

Once I got him settled, all tucked in with a fresh t-shirt because his other was all wet from sweating, I pulled his curtains closed and shut his door. That way he wouldn't hear any of us as we discussed the coins with one another and Grandma Firenzi.

"So, to what do I owe the pleasure of this triple play phone call?"

Vito grabbed his iPad and showed her the screen.

"Can you read this article?" he asked. "If not, we can read it to you and send you the link."

"Give me a minute, honey," she said. "I need my cheaters. Mario, hand me my glasses, will you, sweetheart? They're by the recliner."

In a minute, Mario popped back onto the screen, dangling her eyeglasses in front of her face. Mario looked sunburned from his nose to his chin, but he had a white forehead from his eyebrows up. No doubt, he'd been wearing a baseball cap while he was at the beach or outside doing yard work or playing golf. I'd seen that image before, mostly on PGA golfers on the television. Grams grabbed at them a few times until finally grasping them and resting them on the bridge of her nose.

"Let me see now," she started. "Hmmmmm, a break-in at the Downtown Art Gallery. Hmmmmm. Pirate themed exhibit. Hmmmm. Oh, my."

"See the connection?" Beans clarified.

"I do, dear. Yes, yes. It's obvious, isn't it?"

"Do you know these people, Grams? I mean at the gallery or the exhibitors?"

"As a matter of fact, yes," she admitted. "I know many of them, and the owner of the shop, too. Lovely woman. Very worldly with her art knowledge. She specializes in Asian artifacts, or at least she did before the store was renovated. Has quite a collection herself from Japan, South Korea, Vietnam, China, and Indonesia. Cypress, Turkey, and Thailand, too. Wood carvings and sculptures, jewelry, textiles, you name it. Aubrey is well renown in the country for her knowledge and personal collections."

"Well," I dared to interrupt, "Do you think you can find out who owns these coins?"

Beans didn't mind my asking. I knew from the get-go that she didn't want to keep anything that didn't belong to her, not if they were stolen from somebody else. She had told her grandmother that from the beginning, but Mrs. Firenzi insisted that "finders' keepers, losers' weepers." The older woman along with Mario's support emphasized that the items were found on her property, therefore, they belonged to her with which to do whatever she wanted.

"I already have an idea," Grandma Firenzi said, rolling her eyes, "and if it is who I think it is, I'd rather you keep them. But I'll ring you back in an hour or so after I make a few calls. All right? You going to be free still?"

"Sure," we all said simultaneously, eagerly wanting to hear the answer to our question. We needed closure.

"Okay then. Toodle loo."

"Bye, Grams. Love you."

"Love you, too, honey. Love you all," Grams winked at the three of us.

Staring at the black screen, the three of us were transfixed in time.

I was thinking about the fact that after all the effort and the threat on Beans' life, there went easy money out the window. The girl deserved to sell the valuable coins and have money for herself and her mother. Not that Paulie didn't provide well for the two of them with her ever-busy orange Volvo, personal taxi by day, regular errands car on off hours. She finally sold the other used car that her friends Mud and Zapper gave her from the Pittsburgh area. It was in better shape physically but turned out to be a dud under the hood. Sadly, it took multiple breakdowns outside of JFK Airport in New York City and Philly Airport for her to list it for sale at the Columbus Market. She didn't care what she got for it. "Best Offer" was the sign she plastered on its windshield. If I remembered correctly, she pocketed a few hundred dollars for it, according to Beans.

"Now what?" Beans scooted to the edge of her place on my couch.

"I suppose we wait," I mentioned, hearing my stomach grumble. "Anybody for a snack?"

Vito was already entrenched in more article research and shook his head no. But Beans asked if I had any M and Ms. Preferably, peanut ones. When I told her that I doubted it, she made a stink face at me. Then she willingly added that she'd take anything that resembled chocolate because she was stressed out. I guess she was thinking how her good fortune wasn't going to come to fruition.

Babcia's assembly production of pierogies seemed finished because she was packaging them in eighteen pieces each. Then she had my sister use the black magic marker on the counter to record the date on the white freezer paper. Haddie took considerable pride in blocking her print to be precise and legible. Her ability to write and read took off under her teacher, Mrs. Pencil. The woman knew how to work her magic in her classroom of autistic students. My dad was the only one to meet her on a parent-teacher conference afternoon in the fall, and he was extremely impressed with her classroom environment, her approaches to teaching these special needs children and her love for each and every one of them. There were moments when Haddie would tell us how to do something with her homework that was "the way Mrs. Pencil does it." As Haddie finished each package, she pushed it aside and said, "Clean up. Clean up. Time to clean up."

Scrambling among the many cabinets in the kitchen, I finally located a small cache of Andes chocolate mints. I remembered that Dad brought them home from Shoprite after Christmas because they were marked down. A steal, he called it.

I yelled out to Beans, "Found some Andes mints. You want those?"

"Mmmmm," she said. "Sure. I love those."

I slid the little box off the shelf and dropped them onto the coffee table in front of my favorite girl. In the blink of an eye, she swooped them up, ripped them open and unwrapped one. Once it was in her mouth, she moaned loudly and busied herself unwrapping a second before she was even done.

"Guess they're still fresh," I said.

"Mmmmmm," was all she could reply, having popped a few more in. Her cheeks puffed out like a squirrel as she chewed on every delicious morsel. "These are just what I needed," she spoke while munching.

Then Beans checked her phone in her pocket.

"Grams just texted me," she announced with a drip of chocolate juice appearing at the corner of her mouth.

Brant Hoagland is definitely interested in having his coins returned.

"Well," she said, having read the report out loud to us, "Who is that? And how do I do that? I don't trust shipping them from UPS or FedEx like you did with your camera, Vito. And I'm not about to place them into the mail."

"Maybe you need to fly down to Florida again and hand deliver them," Vito suggested sarcastically, not really meaning it.

She wrote back quickly, asking for her grandmother's suggestion.

No need to worry about that. He's coming to you.

The startled look on Beans' face said it all.

"What?" I asked.

"Grams said that Brant Hoagland is coming here to get them," she gulped with concern.

"That's so weird," I said. "These are only eleven coins of an entire bunch that he has. If he's a collector or big business investor, why's he need them so badly?"

"Don't know," she said and texted back.

A minute later, she read Grandma Firenzi's reply.

Hoagland is a penny-pinching billionaire. A real estate mogul. He's known by everyone down here. Face is plastered all over billboards. Hoagland Houses, the best on the Gulf Coast. People hate him. Not because he has tons of money, but because he's just not a nice man.

"Oh, great!" my girl-next-door exclaimed.

Vito's eyes lifted off his iPad and stared at my neighbor, "Don't worry. Me and B-Man here will protect you. We're your superheroes."

My eyes first consulted his then glanced over at Beans.

"Yeah, like Ironman and Superman," I kidded, but then my tone got serious upon seeing Beans' concerned face. "He's right. The guy sounds like a creep, and I'm not sure what he's up to by coming here, but we've got your six." I pounded the quarterback's fist in the air. "He's probably an old dude anyway, tiny little body that you can knock over with a puff of air."

That made my neighbor laugh, but it didn't stop Beans from nervously plucking three more chocolates from the package, unwrapping them and shoving them through her lips.

Her nervous condition was now making me nervous.

*   *   *   *   *

Paulie was nowhere in sight when we saw a limousine pull up to the curb outside our house. My dad was leaving work in about an hour, so we were eating dinner late. His recovery was remarkable, nothing short of miraculous, so he decided to go into work for a couple of hours. Vito opted to stick around even though his family already ate their lasagna dinner. I knew he was upset that he missed it, but he said he'd settle for leftovers. Being here for Beans was far too important, Besides, he didn't want me to confront this Brant Hoagland guy alone. Both Beans and I gulped down a plateful of potato and cheese pierogies, all slathered in melted butter and sour cream. Haddie, already satisfied with dinner, was in the bathtub, taking a bath while Babcia supervised. That act itself would tie them up for about an hour since my kid sister loved bath nights, playing with her tub toys until the water got cold. Ironically, she wore her pirate's hat, too, in order to play with her floating pirate's ship. She mentioned "cleaning up" again, knowing she was headed for a tub visit. This time of night was magical for her plus soothing and relaxing.

We all stepped a distance from the front window and watched as a tall, bouncer-type man escorted a smaller one up the front steps to Beans' door. The sight was comical, ebony and ivory by contrast, but it was obvious that the larger African American male protectively shielded the real estate mogul.

Our Mill Creek hero was the first to step to my door and open it.

"Can we help you?" his voice was strong and in command.

Vito's stance was steady and strong. His sweatpants clung to his legs while his sneakered feet glued themselves in place. His hands sat on his hips as if to dare both men to make a bad move. He was ready for them. Me, not so much. Beans, too, hovered in my shadow made by the standing lamp nearby.

"Yes," the smaller man said. He moved closer to the porch rail that divided mine from Beans' and Paulie's. "Looking for a Miss Fagioli. Quinn Fagioli. I was told that she lives at this address," his bony finger pointed at the numbers by Beans' door. "Do you know where I can find her?"

With a sudden burst of audacity and courage, Beans stepped forward and passed Vito.

"That would be me," she said, pulling a rubber band from her lint filled pocket. Her hands deftly pulled back her auburn locks and wrapped them tightly into a ponytail. Her appearance paralleled her mother, a picture of strength and no nonsense. "I know why you're here."

Led by the elbow, the tottering old man slowly shuffled down the steps and crept up mine.

Now we had a much closer look at what we were dealing with.

Brant Hoagland had to be in his nineties. His face was weathered by Florida's sunshine, taking its toll on his complexion that appeared leathery and dry like a crocodile's. The tanned tone meant he still spent hours in the sun and didn't do much to protect his skin at all. Height wise, he couldn't have been more than five feet six inches, just a little taller than Beans and much shorter than Vito and me. The oddest part about him was his ivory knee length overcoat, bright purple and white checkered scarf tucked around his neck, matching leather gloves, forest green pants and matching satin slippers. The sight was quirky and eccentric, but I guessed if I were that rich, I wouldn't care what other people thought about how I dressed. I would be all about the comfort. His companion, however, was head to toe in black. Black baseball cap, black leather jacket also to his knees, black pants, black turtleneck, black boots. And on his upper teeth, I caught the glimpse of a gold tooth. Then there was also that menacing tattoo under his right eye, a black widow spider crawling upward. Small with black, grey, and white details, the thing looked three dimensional and too real. It made my skin crawl. The protector stood directly behind Hoagland, watching and waiting our every move.

"May I come in?" his voice seemed warm enough and ultra-polite.

The three of us checked with one another. There was no way we could take on the big bruiser, but Hoagland was an easy target should he attempt to pull anything over on us.

Without a plan, Beans opened the door and welcomed him, in her faux friendly voice.

"No funny business," she warned him with a grin. "And only for a few minutes."

"It's a deal," the old man said, but his voice sounded maniacal.

That concerned me.

And my protective baseball bat was resting upstairs under my bed. My weapon of choice. I was not prepared for this.

EPILOGUE

Brant Hoagland anxiously flopped himself onto the middle of Booger's couch. Once his feet stepped over the threshold and crossed into the foyer, we noticed how he took control of the environment. Needless to say, he wanted to be right on top of his missing doubloons. He couldn't get any closer than where he situated himself.

That's when I nailed him with a barrage of questions. Vito always said that when I was on a one-tracked mind, I sounded like a machine gun spitting bullets nonstop at my opponent. It was an unfair advantage in which I took immense pleasure, now knowing that my deliberate behavior was a pattern. I'd never realized it until my black-haired Adonis pointed it out to me. That was another thing I liked about him. He was as observant as I was.

"So, Mr. Hoagland. How did you get my name? My address? How did you get here so fast today? Why do you want these eleven pieces of silver so badly? You're quite a wealthy member of the Sarasota community from what I hear. You certainly don't need these, not that I care, nor do I want what doesn't belong to me. But surely, these can't hold sentimental value to you. Or maybe I'm wrong. Maybe that's exactly why you want them? Do they have some personal significance to you in your life? Like, did they belong to your father or mother, perhaps?

Maybe, just maybe, your grandfather was a pirate, and he stole these from some place and left them to you, his only grandson?"

The giant land man in the business community of Sarasota County didn't realize what he'd come up against. His body seemed smaller to me as he sat there, face plastered with questions, not answers. I could see it in his face. So, I targeted him again with a second round before he even got a chance to answer any of my previous questions. From what I felt, I was the giant in the room, not his strong-armed comrade, and I was going to win this battle and take him down.

"These pieces of eight - - yes, I know what they are really called, Mr. Hoagland - - are amazingly unique. According to our research, we know that they were minted in Peru and well over four or five hundred years old." My eyes checked the hulking beast of a man near the doorway, making sure he wasn't coming after me or my friends. He didn't bat an eye, and his facial expression was nonexistent. I wasn't sure how to interpret that, and I didn't want to put any of us into harm's way. "But the question is their true value. Reports indicate," I wanted to sound like an authority from a news outlet, "that they can be worth only twenty-five to fifty dollars each, but more if they have documentation from shipwrecks or other evidence of historical events like absconded loot from property acquired during battles."

Mr. Hoagland tossed me a smirk, tugging off his purple gloves, folding them into a neat little ball and stuffing it into his coat pocket. He'd unbuttoned the front, exposing the fringed bottom of his fancy scarf.

"They must hold a great deal of meaning for you to come all the way to Mill Creek, New Jersey, from wherever you live in Sarasota. I'm sure . . ."

His impatience declared itself as he interrupted me, "Young lady. I live on Long Boat Key as if it's any of your business anyway. I have several homes, but that's the one that serves me well at present. It's valued at three million dollars and change, something the likes of you will never see."

Booger couldn't contain himself, "No need to be rude, sir."

Hoagland's head snapped around and his eyes pierced Booger's, "I'm not here to see you, young man. Nor you either," he locked in on Vito. "My business is only with Miss Fagioli here. Perhaps, you two could leave us alone to talk, privately."

Booger began to object, but Vito agreed wholeheartedly. He tugged at my neighbor's arm then the two of them walked out of the room in a huff and headed upstairs to Booger's bedroom.

I was a little taken back by that.

Being alone with the bodyguard and the old man made me more nervous than I thought I could be. I prayed that Booger and Vito were upstairs making a plan just in case we needed to call Chief Rusamano or contact Booger's dad. But my two friends were up there, and I was down here. I had to regroup and keep drilling Hoagland.

"Now, what answers are you willing to share?"

"May I ask for a drink of water?" Brant Hoagland's tone shifted to patient and kind.

But I didn't trust him. I assumed that all his power and money made him used to getting his way. And if I left the room, he'd most likely grab the money and take off. I planned to hand over his property anyway, but I wanted answers before I did that. As if a warning, the gleaming chandelier over Booger's dining room table flickered like indoor lightning.

"In a minute," I muttered, suddenly realizing that his dark green pants were actually part of a set of satin pajamas or loungewear. The button down lapeled top resting under his scarf definitely smacked of ritzy PJs. "But first, answers."

"Young lady," he wiggled forward on the couch cushion, "You are correct about the value of these coins. These 'bare bones' as the pirates called them aren't worth much alone by themselves. But they are as a part of my set, the full exhibit being presented at Downtown Art."

"Yeah, Grams told me that you had a display there."

"Not merely a display, child. One of the largest collections of a famous shipwreck in the world. A notorious event. One that has gained momentum over time. It has no price tag, only a value for history." The frail man patted the thick white hair on his head then lightly traced the matching pencil thin moustache under his nose. "Have you ever heard of pirates of the Caribbean?" his face grew serious as he spoke to me.

Had I ever! Jack Sparrow and I were old friends. I could say, "Thick as thieves," but only I would get the joke. I cracked myself up.

Brant Hoagland summoned his huge gorilla to come to the coffee table. There the stoic man reached inside his coat pocket and withdrew a long, large piece of soiled paper. I could see the visible brown stains spotting it as his black grip released it to Hoagland. He uttered, "Here, boss," then he backed up, retreating to his post like a dedicated sentry.

Hoagland scooted the coins off to the corner beyond him then unfolded the paper. Its size encompassed the entire table, about two feet by four feet. Gently, he pressed his wrinkled, liver spotted hands on the tarnished paper, reminding me of my tea-stained technique for a history project in fifth grade.

"Here is a map of the west coast of Florida, from Charlotte Harbor near Punta Gorda, all the way up to Old Tampa Harbor and Hillsborough Harbor. Here's Alligator Bay and the Peace River, too." He explained as his fingers looped and circled through the spots on the old locations on the Gulf of Mexico. "The unique exhibit that I have at Downtown Art is the largest collection of its kind with pirate treasures and artifacts from Florida. A shipwreck in Charleston Harbor produced many artifacts. But parts of my collection made trips up from the Caribbean, and thefts from the likes of Amara Pargo, Stede Bonnet, Captain Jack Randall, Ann Bonny, and the notorious Jean Laffite."

My eyes pinpointed Sarasota situated between them. And I was shocked to hear the name of a woman.

"From the time I was a child, you were right, Miss Quinn." Calling me Miss Quinn was a common expression in the South, always using the title Miss or Mr. with a person's first name out of respect. "My grandfather got me interested in pirates from the time I was about five years old. He gave me my first doubloons, bartered from another collector who swore they were from a treasure chest buried on Pinellas Point. That's up by Clearwater and St. Petersburg near Tampa. My grandfather did, however, excavate privately around that area when he was in his fifties and found random loot or booty as pirates called it. Pieces of gold wrist cuffs and necklaces got added to his collection along with folklore, and tales of the legendary Jose Gaspar or Gasparilla. Does he ring a bell?"

I shook my head no. Not one of them rang a bell. I knew nothing of pirates except the ones whose costumes hung up in the Halloween shops every October.

"The people of Tampa would frown upon your ignorance, young lady," he laughed with a smarmy grin. "They host a huge parade with the Gasparilla Pirate Festival annually. They reenact pirates attacking the village and stealing their goods. It's a big deal, held at the end of every January." He held his hand up and snapped his fingers. The burly man of muscle again came to life and produced another document. "Here's a picture of Gasparilla. He's a mythical man from all accounts and research. But all the artifacts that I have at the exhibit are real and have been authenticated. There are two hundred twenty-five of them, ranging from currency to jewels to maps to ledger books. All in average to good condition, making the groups collectively valued at over a million dollars."

I studied the drawing closely. The man in the picture had a wind-blown mop of black hair and an accompanying moustache, one whose ends flipped upward in curls. A thin, closely shorn beard hugged his jagged jawline and his eyebrows arched in sharp points above his beaty eyes. The nose at the center of his face was long and jagged, the outcome a result of too many heated punches. Around his neck was a double wrapped scarf. It draped over a plain black shirt with no buttons. Finally, I spotted a round black earring in his left earlobe, perhaps an onyx jewel. No doubt, the gem came from a confiscated cargo ship. From all appearances, Jose Gaspar was, indeed, a scoundrel.

From overhead, I could detect footsteps and furniture moving. My bet was that Vito and Booger were listening to us through the heating vents. I was happy for the subtle reminder that they were still there, keeping an ear on me.

"How long ago did the pirates sail up around those areas?"

"From the 1550s until the early 1800s when explorers began to create settlements in the area. But until then, pirates found refuge in the marshlands and inlets. Those places were easy to access away from the major waterways but handy for quick attacks on major vessels and fleets moving along."

"Geesh, that's a long time!" I gasped. "So, do you think there is still treasure stashed all over those places? I mean deep in the beach sands and everything?"

His fingers latched together and established a spot on his lap, "I'm sure there are. Why? Interested in becoming a pirate?"

"No, nothing like that, but it sure would make sense that not everything has ever been recovered if they stowed it away in secrecy. And especially, if they did it fast, not paying full attention to where they stashed it all. From the way you've explained everything," my tone definitely showed increased interest in something I knew nothing about, "there's plenty more for the taking. Like the gold hidden in Alaska and other parts of our western states."

Without announcement, Brant Hoagland stood up. At the same time, Stan Bugerowski appeared at the front door. Hoagland must have spotted him before us to respond like that. Mr. B.'s face grew alarmed, seeing just me in the room with two odd looking strangers. But I jumped up quickly and made the introductions.

"Oh, hi there, Mr. B. These two gentlemen came to collect some found objects from me," I scurried to his side, thankful to have him come home. Good timing. "Mr. Brant Hoagland. This is Mr. Stan Bugerowski. My neighbor. This is his house. And Mr. B, this here is Mr. . . . . ," but I didn't know the hulking beast's name.

"Bruiser," the wall of a man held out his hand, and Mr. Bugerowski shook it with slight hesitation.

Then there was a rush of footsteps clamoring down the staircase.

"Hiya, Pop," Booger smiled at his dad. His baseball bat was clutched in his left hand. Vito, in turn, also carried a weapon. The heavy black base of Booger's bedroom lamp. Both shade and light bulb removed. "Glad you're home."

"Me, too. I think," the man laughed, an older version of his son with exception to a mop of brown hair. His hair was graying at the temples but there was a lot of it, still being in his late thirties. His white work coat was splattered with blood from the butcher shop in the meat department at Shoprite. But his black pants and work boots were pristine in contrast.

"You still feeling okay, Pop?" his son asked.

"I'm fine, son," the man told him, patting Booger on the back. "Just tuckered out a bit."

Without additional chatter, Hoagland plucked the eleven silver rounds from the table and handed them to Bruiser. The human skyscraper brought out a small change purse from his inside jacket pocket and placed the valuables within. The brown object looked so dinky in the palm of his hand and practically disappeared with his matching skin tone before he tucked it away. My Grams had one just like it but in pink. The sight of such a huge man carting a teeny tiny change purse was nothing short of comical, but I dared not laugh.

"Where are my manners," Mr. Bugerowski said. "Can I get you two anything to drink or a snack?"

Mr. Hoagland remained in his place and began buttoning his coat. Then he readjusted his expensive scarf, making sure to have every piece of it tucked inside, and took out his purple gloves. I caught Mr. B. staring at them because they were a raging royal purple, perhaps to signify Hoagland's status, the King of Real Estate.

"While I appreciate the gesture, I must get back. I'll gladly take a bottle of water to go," he said, waltzing to the front door past Stan. "My helicopter is waiting for me at the Flying W down a ways."

He had a private helicopter?

"It'll get us to my private jet in a hurry. It's at the Philadelphia Airport. I have a late supper waiting for me and a business conference with the members of the Greater Sarasota Chamber of Commerce."

He had a private jet?

My mind was reeling with images of gold on every ounce of the plane, both inside and out. The guy was dripping in moolah. But other than his eccentric style of dress, one would never really know it.

"Hey, just one more question," I dared to step forward, seeking a solution to the cause of the robbery and hideaway at Grams' place. "Who stole these from your display? At the gallery, I mean?"

Hoagland clasped his hands together, "A cleaning lady for the gallery. Her brother knew she had access. Had her open the back doors of the building when she went in for the night shift. Led him directly to the case. There, he jimmied the lock, removed the pieces then used her cleaning solution to remove any evidence of prints. She managed somehow to relock the case and then finished the rest of her cleaning. She forgot, however, to secure the backdoor. Probably, nerves interrupted her routine."

"Let me guess," I said. "Her brother's name was Alvaro."

"Nope, but his cousin's was. They needed money for their roof and tile business and to pay personal bills. The business was just starting up, and they really hadn't planned on how to budget both."

Suddenly, I felt sorry for the workers. Laborers who could never reach the elite status that Hoagland held. Never in their lifetimes.

"But why did they decide to hide the stash at my grandmother's?"

"Convenience," Hoagland adjusted his stance. "Must've been working at your grandmother's place when the heat was on. Made sense to hide them away there until they could come back and finish their work. Taking advantage of a poor, unsuspecting elderly lady, I'm thinking."

Unsuspecting? While it was true that my Grams was elderly, she wasn't naïve. Her only weakness was kindness. She probably trusted the workers to do their job and nothing else, not paying much attention to what they were really up to.

Just before he exited, he again gestured to Bruiser. The bodyguard dug into the other inner pocket of his jacket and withdrew a white business envelope. He handed it to Brant Hoagland who, in turn, handed it to me.

"For your trouble," the man scoffed then was on his way, taking Stan's water bottle along with him.

Bruiser closed the door behind him and quickly moved past the man on the steps so he could open the back door of the limo for his boss. He was a loyal employee throughout the visit, and Mr. Hoagland needed to count his blessings for that.

Mr. Bugerowski snapped into action and immediately locked the door. Then he shrugged at the three of us and headed into the kitchen for his after-work bottle of suds, as he called it, so he could unwind. The entire scene held no interest to him nor any concern. That somewhat surprised me. But then again, he was still overcoming a short illness and a couple hours of work. His brain was probably not thinking clearly.

Vito was first to approach me while Booger was right on his heels.

"Well," they both said in unison. "Aren't you going to open it?"

In truth, I wasn't that interested. The silver doubloons were gone now, and I had hoped to have them as a memory of Grams' burglary case. They had been an unexpected souvenir of my trip to her Florida home. And while it was a scary ordeal, it sure was an exciting new adventure.

I found my way to the dining room table. Satan, now awake from below it, sniffed my feet. Not once had the clumsy black standard poodle stirred while the strangers were in Booger's home. But now, suddenly, he wanted to know what was going on. Carefully, I tucked my index finger under an unglued section of the flap and ripped across the top. Inside was a crisp new fifty-dollar bill. A somber etching of Ulysses S. Grant, our eighteenth president, stared at me from the center of it. I held it up in the air and checked both sides of the paper for a moment. Then I couldn't help myself and let out an uncontrollable laugh. Grams warned me that Hoagland was a cheapskate. This merely sealed the deal, proving it true.

"You're not ticked off?" Booger asked me with a confused look on his face. "I'd be hopping mad!"

"Nah," I said, crumpling up the empty envelope and tossing it onto the table, "I'm just happy we're all here to live another day."

I knew it sounded overdramatic, but it was the truth.

On that note, Haddie came out in her pink bathrobe. Her eye patch was still on and the wet strands on her head were all wrapped up in a unicorn hair wrap. Haddie's slippers were floppy koala bears, their heads at her toes and fuzzy tail at her heels. The swashbuckling sword sliced the air above her. She was quite a sight to behold.

"Arrrrrr," she snarled at us. "Cleaned up," she smiled.

Suddenly, she made sense. Somehow, she knew the details of the case, most likely from overhearing me and Booger and Vito through visits and phone calls. She surmised that a cleaning crew at the art gallery might've been involved. And she was right. We just hadn't put two and two together. The clever little girl was a few steps ahead of us. Booger would seek more answers from his kid sister in days to come, accepting that her intuition was a gift.

I waved the fifty-dollar bill in front of us, thinking it could be counterfeit. I didn't trust that Hoagland guy. And it would be just like him to get the last laugh.

"Yes, we cleaned up, Haddie."

Our disappointment immediately turned into laughter.

And we recognized how we valued one another, more than Spanish doubloons.

Friends and families. The best treasures of all.

ARTIFACTS

Jose Gaspar, legendary pirate nicknamed Gasparilla from the Pinellas County area of western Florida, supposedly lived in the late 18th century to the early 19th century. According to legend, he terrorized the southwest coast of Florida until he leapt to his death from his ship rather than facing capture by the United States Navy. All of his treasure has yet to be fully discovered. There are no court records, ship logs, newspapers or other archives that document his existence. An inn owner on Gasparilla Island promoted a fictional biography of the man and swore there was no truth in it at all, but others beg to differ. (Information and photo from Carolyn Arnold's *The Legend of Gasparilla and His Treasure*, 2020)

These doubloons are authentic and privately owned by a coin collector in North America. The front of the doubloon holds the Coat of Arms of the Hapsburg royal family. It is known as the Hapsburg Shield. King Ferdinand and Queen Isabella of Spain who funded Christopher Columbus' journey to America were a part of the Hapsburg royal family. The Crusader's Cross appeared on the back of the coins. It symbolized the close tie between the government of Spain and the country's Catholic religion. The lion and the castle frequently appear on the reverse of the coin, too. These symbolize the provinces of Leon and Castille in northwestern Spain, bordered by the country of Portugal. ("History of the Spanish Doubloon." Retrieved from The Northwest Territorial Mint on April 27, 2022. https:/www.newmint.com)

This map is a replica of an original that combines various markings and indicated locations of treasures absconded or hidden in and around the coast of Florida and neighboring islands. The "X" marks the spot identifies places where pirates confiscated cargo or where shipwrecks occurred. All of these are noteworthy because Spanish reales or doubloons were part of shipments on Spanish vessels. These all date back to the 1500s. (Map retrieved from author's library)

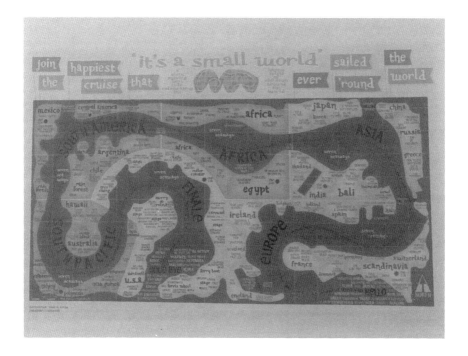

A map of the attraction, "It's a Small World" in Fantasyland at Walt Disney World in Orlando, Florida. The map displays the waterway journey through the countries of the world, complements of Magic Kingdom for paying guests in 2014. The attraction first appeared at Disneyland Park in Anaheim, California, in 1966, after its debut at the World Fair in New York City. (Map retrieved from author's souvenir collection from Walt Disney World parks)

STUDY GUIDE QUESTIONS

1. At the beginning of the story, Beans is going to take her first airplane ride. How does she feel about it? Have you ever been on an airplane to travel somewhere? What do you remember about your experience and how you felt?

2. Have you or someone close to you ever found an item that does not belong to you? What was it and what did you do with it? Why doesn't Beans immediately try to find the rightful owner once she discovers the revealed doubloons?

3. What is a fair-weather friend versus a BFF? Which do you have and how do you know?

4. Two new vocabulary words that you might have learned are "frugal" and "spendthrift." Which would you prefer to be? Explain your choice.

5. Sarasota, Florida, where Grandma Firenzi lives, is quite different from Mill Creek, New Jersey, where Beans and her mother Paulie live. List several of these differences.

6. What is a lanai? What do houses in New Jersey and other states have that are similar? What purpose do all of them serve?

7. We discover that Beans also has never been to an amusement park or a place of attractions for the family like Walt Disney World in Orlando. But once she experiences a few rides, she

finds great enjoyment out of each one. What amusement parks have you visited? What favorite rides did you enjoy? Explain.

8. How does Beans' misadventure at *The Pirates of the Caribbean* ride compare to Booger's boardwalk experience at the seashore last summer?

9. How and why did Booger change his mind about Colin Malloy? What did Officer Wallace make false assumptions about regarding Booger and Malloy's car?

10. Babcia, Booger's Polish grandmother, is a main caretaker for little Haddie and Booger along with her son Stan. Babcia has lived with Booger and his father Stan Bugerowski for four years now. In what ways does she seem "Americanized" yet still preserve her Polish roots?

11. Brant Hoagland is a real estate mogul. What does that mean? How is his physical size the direct opposite of his successful career?

12. Many of the characters in the story enjoy hobbies. Name a few. What type of hobbies or special interests do you have?

13. Forensic science is a critical part of investigations in today's police work. What is forensic science? What kind of equipment does Vito use in this story to help him investigate and collect data?

14. Authors frequently use figurative language to aid the reader with understanding a character, the environment / setting, and the plot. Search through the chapters and find at least ten different examples. Label them if you can. (For example, personification = the tree's branches waved at us in the ferocious wind; alliteration = my mother muttered a comment at me; simile = Haddie shot like a bullet through the dining room to the

kitchen; or metaphor = Inside the dark ride became nighttime during the day.)

15. What is an art gallery? What is a boutique? Many of these places exist in cities and towns that host larger sized populations. Does the town or city where you live have either or both? Share with a friend.

16. Have you ever read books or stories about pirates from the past? What do you know about them? There are pirates still today, but they operate differently. What kind of pirates are they, what do they do and where do they attack?

17. Explain what you know about the Spanish dollar and "pieces of eight." How are the two related and used? What type of coin currency that we use in the United States today comes closest to doubloons?

QUESTIONS AND ANSWERS

This section is a little different this time. Most of these questions came from an "Icebreaker Game" with the students from Gloria M. Sabater Elementary School in Vineland, New Jersey. When I visited Ms. Jackie Farside's 5th grade class in the school year 2021-2022, March 2022 ("Read Across America" month), they asked fascinating questions and probed for answers, from the easiest to the hardest. Students tried to guess the answers before I shared my personal facts. I appreciated them playing along and they added some flavorful questions of their own. The following includes a mixture of all of them:

Q. What is your favorite color?
A. Orange. Many thought it was red, but that was a tie for second place along with powder blue.

Q: How many times have you flown on an airplane?
A: Probably four dozen times or more. Most were trips domestically or around our country. My friends, husband and family went to places like Washington, California, Nevada, South Dakota, New Hampshire, Massachusetts, Texas, Florida, North Carolina, South Carolina, Tennessee, Ohio. Pennsylvania, and Indiana. Other places were trips by car, often driving long distances. I think I've visited all the states but five. Oh, and I flew a short jaunt to skydive, too, but that was a trip of a whole other sort.

Q. Have you ever traveled out of the country?

A. Yes, I've been to many countries outside of the United States. The first long plane trip I had was when I was an American Youth Exchange student in the summer of 1967. I flew to Miami, Florida, first to connect with a flight to Santiago, Chile. (I lived in Vina del Mar with a Chilean family for thirteen weeks. Such a wonderfully enlightening experience, and my Spanish speaking abilities after two years of high school study really developed.) Before that, my family visited Canada and I returned there with my boyfriend at the time (now my husband John) to tour Montreal. When I taught high school in Haddonfield, New Jersey, colleagues, and I chaperoned juniors and seniors to places like England, Scotland, Ireland, and Wales. My immediate family and I took several trips abroad between 1999 and 2005; these included England, Scotland, Italy, Spain, and Morocco. In addition, my son and his wife got married in Jamaica so, of course, we traveled there, and my husband and I vacationed with dear friends in Costa Rica. The sum hits eleven. I never counted before. Phew! That's fairly good. I'm hoping to still visit more on my bucket list.

Q. What is your favorite movie?

A. *The Wizard of Oz.* As a child growing up, both your teacher and I watched it on television around Thanksgiving time. There were plenty of commercials, but we loved watching the movie turn from black and white to color. When I was little, all our television shows were in black and white until the 1960s. That's when my parents could afford to buy our first color television set. My own children one time asked me if we were poor because my family didn't have color TVs, so I had to explain to them that there weren't any color

TVs back then. They felt bad for me. So cute, but they didn't understand at that early age when they asked me.

Q. If you had the opportunity to go to the moon, would you?
A. Yes, if it was totally funded and full proof in safety features. Space has always intrigued me, and I still remember the first astronauts who traveled around the moon and the ones who took their first steps after landing on its surface. Watching it on television in real time was amazing and mind boggling.

Q. Who is your favorite actor?
A. One you might have heard of is Meryl Streep. (The class hadn't.) She's a marvelously talented lady who can play any character, no matter how funny or how serious. It's as though her body morphs into a whole different human being than who she really is. (I had to explain the word morph then added that Meryl Streep was the mother in the movie musical, *Mama Mia*, and the witch in the movie musical *Into the Woods*. None of it helped. Too funny.)

Q. What's your favorite TV show?
A. I like game shows and mysteries, but I also love "The Amazing Race" because the contestants get to travel around the world and play games.

Q. How old are you?
A. Ms. Farside told the young man who asked this question that it wasn't polite to ask such a question to an older person. But I told them I was older than a 55-mph speed limit. (Later another boy, trying to be clever and figure it out, asked me in what year I was born. I said in the 1950s. That seemed to satisfy him.)

Q. What are your favorite foods?

A. Homemade pizza, Mexican chimichangas or tacos, Greek sou-vlaki, and moussaka, plus anything Italian (lasagna, ravioli, sausage, and peppers). I'm also partial to a plain old hot dog with chopped raw onion, sauerkraut, and mustard. (There were quite a few groans over that answer.)

Q. Which one of your books is your favorite?

A. That's a tough question to answer because they all hold a spe-cial place in my heart. Sometimes it's because of the storyline that reflects real history or a current event taken from a headline. Other times, it's because of the type of mystery it is and the twists the plot takes.

Q. Which do you like better – the mountains or the beach?

A. The beach or the shore, like we say in New Jersey.

Q. What are your favorite hobbies?

A. Reading, watching movies, dancing, bike riding and walking (for exercise)

Q. What household chore do you dislike the most?

A. I hate cleaning the house. It's a never-ending job.

Q. Do you have any pets?

A. Not anymore. We lost our English Springer Spaniel in 2005 and decided not to have another dog. When I was little, I had a para-keet and a German Shepherd named Smokey. Both dogs were bred as pedigrees and had long full names. Smokey Von Edelhaus was out German Shepherd, and Chocolate Chip of Deerbrook was our spaniel, but we called him Chipper or Chip. When my daughter and son-in-law must be out of town for a while, we watch their Beagle-German Shepherd mix. Her name is Sookie, and she's the best "grand-doggie" ever.

Q. Is it hard to write a book?

A. It's not that it's hard as much as it is developing an idea, and since I love writing mysteries, I must keep producing new cases that have to be investigated and solved. Everything must fall into place. And my books are in a series so that means I have reoccurring characters. I need to track their information to be sure the books parallel their prior facts. (Showed them my notebook with baseball card sleeves, one per character.) If I need to review a character who hasn't been in a book in a while, I must consult those index cards.

Q. What did you want to be when you grew up?

A. All three of those mentioned (lawyer, teacher or librarian, cowboy, and actor). But from the time I was a toddler until about second grade, I wanted to be a cowboy, I wanted to ride a horse all over my hometown, wear boots, a hat, and the whole works. Once I got into high school, I sincerely considered being a lawyer or a librarian then a teacher and an actor. I have fulfilled the dream of being in a classroom, having taught middle school ages, high school and now college (teaching and training new teachers). I also have a SAG-AFTRA (Screen Actors Guild and American Federation of Television and Radio) card that allows me to work on films, television, nonfiction commercial work and radio, and I have been in a variety of those since high school and college.

Q. What famous people have you worked with in movies or TV?

A. Too many to list them all, but a few that you might know are Bradley Cooper, Sarah Jessica Parker (if you saw the movie *Hocus Pocus*, she was one of the witches), Mark Wahlberg, Adam Ruck (he was Cameron in the Ferris Bueller film), and a ton more. Most of them were great to work with, friendly to everyone and respectful.

Q. How many children do you have and grandchildren?

A. I have two adult children who are married with children of their own. My daughter lives near me with her husband and my grandson Cameron who is two and a half years old. My son lives in Florida with his wife and my two granddaughters, Evelina who is almost six and Fiona who is almost four and a half. We love them all very much.

Q: You mention that Grams and Paulie love history, and that Beans is beginning to have a growing interest and appreciation of it, too. Is that a characteristic that you share with them?

A: Yes. So many of my books hinge on historical events, ones I've always known about from schooling but ones that I've grown to discover through research or location visits over my years of vacationing. For example, when I attended my public elementary school, my eighth-grade class took our graduation trip to New York City, Flushing Meadows in Queens specifically, where I experienced *It's a Small World* and my first Belgian Waffle.

Q. What book are you working on now?

A. One that has a connection to pirates. That's all I can tell you. You'll have to wait until it comes out this summer and read it.

Q: You spend many hours either hosting or speaking to various children and adult groups around your region. What types of things do you bring to those conversations?

A. Several years ago after I wrote the Zombie book, I did a presentation at my old high school in Florence, New Jersey. Now, however, it is called The Riverfront School and hosts a combined middle school and upper elementary grades. When I spoke to the older students, one boy (Jake) asked me if I ever have a superhero in my stories. I asked, "Like who?" Kiddingly, he suggested an original one named Banana-man. The idea stuck with me, so I took him up on the idea and wrote that character into one of my following novels.

A SPECIAL NOTE

At this point, I offered for students to "help me write" part of my book. I showed them photos of the attraction, *Its's a Small World,* in Walt Disney World and asked them to describe what they observed with new and unique word choices. The following bold, underlined words and passages denote many of their contributions:

From Chapter 7

prepared to enter a big boat. **One approached, all blue and wooden, but it looked like it was covered in oil**. Packed full of adults and kids alike, we couldn't help but notice **their expressions** of complete satisfaction. Each vessel had five rows and seemed to hold around twenty people.

As we floated through the murky water, **the sky darkened**. To the right, bright whites and silvers and blue hues welcomed us. The Cast Member was one hundred per cent correct. There was so much to view that my eyes felt like they were popping out of my head. Right from the get-go, **doll-like children** were singing,

"I think **India was my favorite** with its Taj Mahal and flying carpets," Mom shared with the two of us as we headed to the dock, "and the giraffes and monkeys plus all those **brightly colored, different flowers** in Africa."

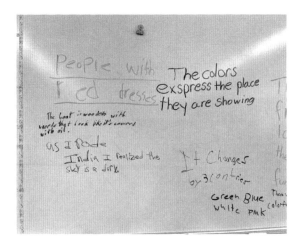

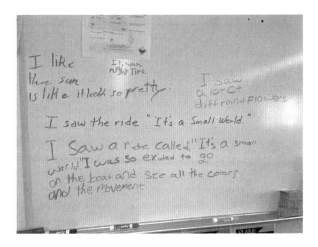

Ms. Jackie Farside's 5th Grade Class at Gloria M. Sabater Elementary School in Vineland, New Jersey, worked diligently and shared writing ideas for both concepts and descriptions in Chapter Seven: Making A Splash. They did diligence to their observations and cautiously selected words to identify what they saw. We had a wonderful time collaborating, a different lesson learned in the writing curriculum. Congratulations to the budding writers.

This photo introduces Ms. Jackie Farside and her fifth-grade students. In March 2022, the State of New Jersey lifted its mandate on masks (post-covid pandemic), but many students and teachers continued to wear them as an option when I visited the classroom at their school. They are holding their "book gifts" and eagerly awaiting reading time with them, a celebration of Read Across America month.

ACKNOWLEDGEMENTS

There are never enough words that can capture my gratitude and thanks to all the people who help me through my newest book journey. By far, number one of my list are the members of my immediate family - Cassandra, Seth, and Cameron; Kirk, Melanie, Evelina, and Fiona; my husband John; my mother Hedgie (Helen); and my sisters Trish and Kathy with their families. Their continuous support and encouragement carries me through the toughest days on the computer keyboard. I also wish to thank my special copy editors, Melanie, Debbie, Chris and Kelly for their "hawk eyes" in combing through the manuscript, a tedious job that they do with love – their recommendations, questions and suggestions are sincere and welcomed at every turn; the consortium of readers from Saints Francis and Clare Parishes and Holy Assumption Church in Roebling, New Jersey; cover artist and dear cousin Deborah Powell of Fort Collins, CO, who always stops what she's doing to consider what materials she has or needs (in her collective arsenal of artist goodies) to complete another illustrative interpretation of my words and world for each book; selective art galleries and art boutiques around Burlington County who discussed their security equipment and protocol for intruders; Medford Township Police Department for their counsel on dispatch and responses to break-ins; the magnificent and rewarding parks of Walt Disney World in Orlando, Florida, especially Magic

Kingdom; talk show hosts Dennis Malloy and Judi Franco – the 10AM to 2PM time slot - of NJ 101.5 for their ongoing support and "shout outs" on the air; Fort Steuben in Steubenville, Ohio, whose gift shop honors my mystery series; and finally,, the Society of Children's Book Writers and Illustrators, especially our New Jersey division. Additional gratitude to the Chambers of Commerce in Pinellas County, Florida, and other local officials of the area. Finally, I thank my readers, in particular, the students with whom I've Zoomed or Skyped or visited in person. Of the latter, I am especially grateful to Ms. Jackie Farside's 5th grade students at Gloria M. Sabater Elementary School SY 2021-2022 in Vineland, New Jersey – their creative offerings in Chapter Seven made writing that chapter a unique and heartwarming treat for me. These students, who visited Walt Disney World's "It's a Small World" ride attraction in Fantasyland, Magic Kingdom, for the first time via my power point presentation, used their keen observations to share selective, descriptive wording. They include the following: Yvonne Abreu Rodriguez, Ariel Arroyo, Evadaisy Barcenas Ramirez, Randy Bautista Trejo, Christopher Bernal-Zaldivar, Rafael Castillo, Jesus Cruz Gonzalez, Ashley Escobar De La Cruz, Emmany Espinal Sanchez, Aaron Flores, Luis Francisco Sanchez, Ja'Siah Jenkins, Hera Jimenez Jarquin, Daniela Lopez Rodriguez, Arlette Martinez Ramirez, Kaylee Perez, Jeaneth Perez Vargas, Giovani Primero, Joaquin Quintero, Liliana Reyes, Joel Rodriguez, Allisson Rodriguez Soto, Ashley Rojas Martinez, Heidy Ruiz and Ismael Sinaca Beteta. Among them, no doubt, are budding authors who will write for our future entertainment.

AUTHOR

Ali LaVecchia is the author of the MG (Middle Grade) Booger and Beans Mystery Series. Her first book *The Case of the White Knight* received "5 Stars out of 5 Stars" on Good Reads followed by *Mystery at Mill Creek Bridge* and *A Zombie on Peacock Hill,* respectively. Ali continues the series with *A Treasure in Satan's Knoll, The Case of the Mascot's Missing Fire, Voices Beyond the Hidden Staircase, The Ghost on the Front Porch, The Secret in the Old Scrapbook* and *The Case of the Vanishing Mail.*

For thirty-two years, Ali worked as a high school and middle school English, Acting, Public Speaking, Creative Writing and Film teacher. She also served as a department facilitator and Director of Curriculum and Instruction in NJ public school districts. During those years, Ali directed over sixty-one plays and musicals and served as advisor and coach of Drama Club, Peer Leadership and World AIDS Alliance. Since 1991, Ali presented several writing projects at the National Council Teachers of English (NCTE) conventions and appeared in the organization's publications. Her poetry has been showcased at the annual Geraldine R. Dodge Poetry Festival, too.

She is a New Jersey native who lives in a suburb of Philadelphia with her husband John. Her days are filled with teaching in the Master of Arts in Teaching program for Fairleigh Dickinson University (mentoring, training and field supervising new as well as veteran teachers, K-12), acting as a SAG-AFTRA member in regional films and television, and, of course, writing more mysteries, starring Booger and Beans. Currently, Ali is also seeking publishers for three children's picture books, two women's fiction novels and a nonfiction MG book on Dr. James Still, historic herbologist and black doctor of the Pines.

With any extra time, Ali enjoys worldwide travels, countryside bike rides and time with her adult children and granddaughters Evelina and Fiona plus grandson Cameron.

COMING SOON:

A SNEAK THIEF IN THE SHADOWS

When the students at Mill Creek Middle School return from Winter Break, a sudden rash of thefts begin. Beans only becomes aware of the suspicious robberies when her locker is ransacked and her lucky rabbit's foot, gone. She depends on that fuzzy favorite, especially on test days. But now, the spot where it sat on the top shelf of her locker is empty. She rifles through her notebooks above and her books below, but her lucky talisman is nowhere to be seen. When Beans mentions the incident to Drew at lunch, her friend confesses that she, too, is a victim, having had her new sneakers stolen the day before from her gym locker. Beans reports the incidents to the new principal, Mrs. Mancini, at the risk of being called a *snitch* then volunteers to get to the bottom of the mysterious disappearances.